Edmund Hodgson Yates

Castaway

A Novel: Vol. I.

Edmund Hodgson Yates

Castaway
A Novel: Vol. I.

ISBN/EAN: 9783337043711

Printed in Europe, USA, Canada, Australia, Japan

Cover: Foto ©Andreas Hilbeck / pixelio.de

More available books at **www.hansebooks.com**

A Novel.

By EDMUND YATES,

AUTHOR OF 'NOBODY'S FORTUNE,' 'DR. WAINWRIGHT'S PATIENT,'
'WRECKED IN PORT,' ETC.

'Like some forlorn and desperate castaway.' *Tit. And.*

IN THREE VOLUMES.

VOL. I.

LONDON:

CHAPMAN AND HALL, 193 PICCADILLY.

1872.

To Shirley Brooks.

Just eighteen years ago, I read in the *Morning Chronicle* some kind words about a story in verse which I had contributed to the *Keepsake*, and which was the first composition of mine that attained the dignity of publication. Those kind words I found, on inquiry, were written by you; since then they have been followed by many kind deeds.

In very slight acknowledgment of our long friendship, I inscribe this Book to you.

EDMUND YATES.

London, January 1872.

CONTENTS OF VOL. I.

———◦✦◦———

Prologue.

Book the First.

CASTAWAY.

Prologue.

CHAPTER I.

AFTER MESS.

'Just fetch my coat out of the commercial-room, Sam, and get my luggage ready for the bus—I am going by the eight-forty-five.'

'Is this yours, Mr. Baines?' said the person addressed, the boots of the hotel, pointing to a number of queer-looking packages wrapped in leather, and secured with huge straps and buckles, which were lying in the passage of the George Inn at Cheeseborough.

VOL. I.   B

'Yes,' replied Mr. Baines; 'you ought to know, you have seen them often enough.'

'Well, do you know,' said the boots slowly, 'I daresay you may think it odd, but there is a good deal of luggage of the same pattern as is brought to this house. The fancy line ain't what it was, Mr. Baines.'

'You are right, Sam,' said Mr. Baines, 'it's overdone, it's— Hallo! what's that?' he cried, as a roar of laughter rang through the house. 'Got a public dinner going on, Sam?'

'No, not exactly,' said Sam. 'Yeomanry's out, and a fine out they are making of it. There is six hundred of them in one place and another up and down the town; and there has been a review to-day, and the officers has been dining here afterwards. That was them hallooing just now.'

'Yeomanry, eh!' said Mr. Baines. 'I don't hold much with yeomanry, Sam; my idea is that the proper way to defend this country—'

But Mr. Baines was compelled to postpone his intention of imparting his notions for the national defence, as at that moment

the omnibus drove up, and seeing in it a
representative of the rival house of Peto and
Wiggins, Mr. Baines hastened to climb the
box with the view of learning all about the
intended movements of his brother commer-
cial.

Meanwhile the stout Major, whose jokes,
principally levelled against himself, had
evoked the laughter thus commented upon,
had brought his speech to a humorous conclusion, and sat down amid the applause of
his comrades. The disinclination for more
oratory, and the desire to smoke, now im-
pelled most of the officers to push away their
chairs and adjourn to the billiard-room; no
one, however, ventured to move, until the
president, Lieutenant-Colonel Goole — a tall,
handsome man, wearing the Crimean and Indian medals — had risen from his seat, and
bidding his brother officers good-night, and
bowing right and left, had left the room.

Then all restraint was thrown off, everybody began talking to everybody else, caps
and shakoes were hastily donned, and the

doors being thrown open by the waiters, the crowd of young men surged into the passage, and thence into the billiard-room, while some, more highly favoured than the rest, sought the snuggery behind the bar, and there entertained themselves with flirting with the good-looking barmaids.

Only two men remained in the room where the dinner had been held. Both were middle-aged, but one had retained his figure, and a certain unmistakable soldier-like smartness, while the other, close verging on corpulency, unbuttoned his jacket and flung himself back in his chair, with an air of one accustomed to subordinate everything to his sense of personal comfort.

His companion watched these proceedings with a certain amount of curiosity, and when they were completed said, with a laugh:

'By Jove, Jack, this'll never do! If you go on like this you will have to pay three hundred pounds for a charger to carry you. This all comes of selling out early, and going in for domesticity and gentleman-farming.'

'Upon my word I believe you are right, Cleethorpe. I must ride close upon sixteen stone now, and it seems to me that I am putting on flesh every year. I think you are wrong about the selling out though. I could not have stood that confounded " stables" much longer; and as for the domesticity, I was meant to be a home bird, and not a battered old London rake like you.'

'Exactly,' said Captain Cleethorpe, lighting a cigar and handing his case to his friend, 'exactly; the only wonder is to me ·that you still remain in this regiment.'

'Well, you see, Cleethorpe,' said his companion, slowly expelling his smoke, 'there is nothing that I know of so good that you cannot have a little too much of it, and I find that to come down here to see you, my old chum of so many years' standing, and to talk with the Colonel, who is a deuced nice gentlemanly fellow and a man of the world, and to mix with these young fellows, who show me what the present generation is like, does me good by rubbing off the rust—'

He stopped as the door opened, and a young man entered the room. A man a little above the middle height, and apparently not more than eighteen years of age, with a small and singularly well-shaped head and handsome regular features. So handsome was he, with his dark blue eyes and dark chestnut hair, which curled in natural and most unusual ripples over his head, that even men, who are generally accustomed to scorn anything like personal beauty in one of their own sex, were fain to admit that he was good-looking. Artists found his lips too full, and his forehead a little too narrow, but principally admired the shape of his head, and the way in which it was joined to his throat, which they pronounced classical and Byron-like, though they complained that the delicate tints of his complexion were too essentially feminine.

There was, however, nothing effeminate in the young man's manner. He strode into the room without swagger indeed, but with perfect manly ease, and walked up to the far end of the table where he had been sitting during dinner.

'Come to hunt for my cigar-case,' he said, as he passed his two brother officers; 'must have dropped it under the table. O, here it is. Not coming to the billiard-room, Captain Cleethorpe? Do come, there is great fun going on; just going to get up a pool, Captain Norman, and must have you; capital thing for you after dinner. I'll be your player, and take care you have plenty of exercise in walking after your ball.'

And before either of them could reply, he had laughed and quitted the room.

'That's a cheeky youth,' said Captain Norman, looking after him; 'cheeky, but deuced good-looking. One of the new lot, isn't it? Which; not Travers?'

'No,' said Cleethorpe. 'Travers is the great hulking fellow that sat within two of you just now; this lad's name is Heriot. His father is an old army man, now a Major-general and a K.C.B., who has been out in India all his life, and has just retired from

the service. Goole is an old chum of his,
which accounts for the lad being with us,
though I think I understood he is going into
the regulars.'

' The cub is deuced good-looking,' said
Captain Norman, 'but he'll want a good deal
of licking into shape.'

' I don't think that,' said Captain Cleethorpe ; 'he is only a boy, you see, and
cheeky as most boys are, but his manners
are generally pretty enough. The sort of
boy I think I should be proud of,' said the
Captain, slowly puffing at his cigar. 'I wonder what Sir Geoffry will think of him? The
lad hasn't seen his father, he tells me, since
he was a baby.'

' What was it I heard about this old Heriot ?' said Captain Norman ; 'something, I
know; a tremendous martinet, wasn't he?'

' Yes,' said Cleethorpe ; 'when I saw him
out in India he was a strict disciplinarian
and a first-class soldier. Kimandine Heriot
they used to call him out there, from some
wonderful exploit of his in either attacking or

holding—I forget which—some pass during
the Sikh war. But Goole, who, as I say,
knows him very well, was telling me some
other things about him the other day. It
appears when he was last at home he married a goodish-looking woman with money
and position, and that sort of thing, and
everybody thought he would go on the retired list; but he didn't. After some little
time he went out to India again, leaving her
behind him, and she and this boy lived together till she died, about ten years ago, and
since then he has been educated in France.
That's what Goole told me.'

'Devilish interesting story,' said Captain
Norman, who was very nearly asleep, and
roused himself with a start. 'Now let's go
and have a pool.' And he pushed aside his
chair, and stretched himself as he rose.

'All right,' said Captain Cleethorpe, rising
at the same time; and the two officers walked
off together.

CHAPTER II

IN THE BILLIARD-ROOM.

'NICE atmosphere this,' said Captain Cleethorpe to his companion, as he opened the
door of the billiard-room, and walked into a
perfect vapour-bath of tobacco smoke.

'Yes,' said Captain Norman, waving his
hand to and fro before him, in the vain attempt to clear some of the smoke away;
'rather glad I am not going home to-night—
it clings about you so confoundedly, and the
smell of stale smoke is the only one thing
that Mrs. Norman makes a row about. She
don't mind it fresh, but hates it when it is
stale.'

'Ah!' said Cleethorpe, 'then it won't do
for you ever to bring her to see me at the

Bungalow; our parson's wife tells me my place smells just like the inside of a pipe, and she ought to know, for the padre can never put his sermon together on a Saturday without his meerschaum in his mouth. It's clearing off now a bit, or we are getting accustomed to it. Let us see who are here.'

The billiard-room at the George was a very large one, containing two tables—one at either end, and flanked all round the wall by stout horse-hair seats. Billiards were an institution in Cheeseborough; the town had produced one of the most celebrated professional players; and no matter what might be the season of the year, the room at the George was always well filled. The town itself was split into two political parties, hating each other with undying animosity, and keeping up their antagonism not merely at election times, or other periods of political excitement, but throughout the whole year. Each party had its head-quarters; the Liberals at the George and the Conservatives at the Royal, and all banquets, balls, fancy fairs, and public meetings of any kind in which the leaders of either party were interested, took place at one or other of their respective houses.

A Liberal elector of Cheeseborough would as soon have thought of smacking his lips over a glass of senna prepared for him by Mr. Tofts, the chemist, as of whetting his appetite with sherry-and-bitters at the Royal. A Conservative, if he could have imagined himself ordering such a draught, would not have been surprised to find death in the soda-and-brandy mixed for him by the barmaid at the George. But there was no billiard-room at the Royal, and as the game of billiards was a necessity both for Conservatives and Liberals, the billiard-room at the George was looked upon as a kind of neutral ground where they might meet together in friendly union, and where any reference to politics was rigidly tabooed. As happens not unfrequently, some of the keenest local politicians were the most energetic supporters of the game, and it was to their credit that they met night after night, without ever permitting themselves even a reference to the subjects which they discussed so acrimoniously at all other times and places.

On the evening in question the billiard-room was even more full than usual; both tables were occupied, the one with a game of pool, in which most of the officers, and some of the visitors who had been present at the officers' mess, were engaged, the other by a match keenly contested by four of the best players amongst the townspeople. All along the seats ranged round the wall were men in various lounging attitudes, watching the play, and discussing the merits of the players with perfect freedom, or talking over various occurrences of that day's review, at which most of them had been present.

'Goole's not here, I suppose?' said Norman, as they seated themselves at the upper end of the room; 'at least I have not come across him yet.'

'No,' said Cleethorpe; 'he cleared off for home at once; this sort of thing won't do for him.'

'Don't he like tobacco smoke?'

'O, it isn't that a bit — like most old Indians, he's seldom without a cheroot in his mouth — but the fact is, Goole is a very strict disciplinarian, and, having passed the greater part of his life in the command of niggers and natives, he finds it difficult to understand this kind of material,' said Cleethorpe, motioning with his cigar to some of the yeomanry who were standing at the farther table.

'He's like your old friend Heriot, that you were speaking of—a bit of a martinet?'

'Well, yes,' said Cleethorpe. 'He doesn't seem to understand that this is a quasi-volunteer service, and that these men, who give up a certain amount of their time and money— though I allow it is to them amusement—are not to be treated as mere privates in the Line. For instance, Goole would think it quite derogatory to sit in this room while men in the regiment were so far forgetting the respect due to him as to play billiards in his august presence.'

'Perhaps the Major thinks so too?' said Norman; 'as he has taken himself off, and you are the senior officer left to us.'

'The Major has taken himself off because he has discussed one bottle of sherry and two bottles of claret, and makes it a rule never to take spirits after good wine,' said Cleethorpe ; 'and, moreover, I do not intend my dignity as senior officer to prevent my enjoying myself. What do you say; shall we join the next pool?'

'No,' said Norman lazily. 'I am tired after all that bumping about this morning ; besides those young fellows make such a tremendous row. Let's talk to some of these yokels.'

'Well, Mr. Martin,' said he, turning to a stout man in a suit of dark gray, who was sitting next him; 'were you at the review to-day?'

'I were, indeed, Captain, and a main fine sight it was.'

'How did you think your boy Tom looked, Martin?' asked Captain Cleethorpe. 'I told you the riding-master would make something of that seat of his.'

'Well, sir,' said farmer Martin, 'may be 'tis right in the military fashion to hold your heels down and turn your toes out, as if you were at dancing-school, and to jolt about in your saddle like one sack of flour in a large wagon; but that wouldn't do for cross-country work, Captain; you must shorten your stirrup-leathers there.'

'Ay, ay,' said Cleethorpe, nodding. 'By the way, didn't you say you wanted to speak to me this evening, Martin?'

'Yes, sir,' said the old man, dropping his voice, and edging up confidentially towards Captain Cleethorpe. 'It's about Mr. Travers, sir; that tall gentleman with the cue in his hand now.'

'I see. Don't point; he's looking at you,' said Cleethorpe.

'No offence, sir,' said Martin. 'But this Muster Travers, Tom's in his troop, sir, and he du worry Tom's life out.'

'Stop, stop, Martin, I cannot hear this,'

said Captain Cleethorpe hurriedly; 'I cannot listen to complaints of this kind, at all events at such a time, and in such a place. If you have anything to complain of, or rather if your son has anything to complain of against Mr. Travers, he must bring it forward in a proper manner before the Colonel. Did you hear that?' continued Cleethorpe, turning to his friend. 'Not a very popular youth is Mr. Travers, I suspect.'

'Ill-conditioned brute,' said Captain Norman; 'quarrelsome, cantankerous, low-bred lout; a complete specimen of what these young fellows call, in their modern slang, "bad form."'

'He must be a singularly bad lot,' said Cleethorpe, 'for he even managed to-day to have a row with the Major, which I should have thought an impossibility. Hallo! what's that?' He pointed as he spoke to the other end of the room, where a little knot of men were gathered together.

Above the hum arising round them, a thick voice was heard saying, in coarse, com-

mon tones, 'Can't you stand still? Always
jumping about in that infernal French fashion,
like a dancing-master! That's the second time
you have spoiled my stroke!'

'That's that brute Travers, by the voice,'
said Norman, raising himself up on his elbow,
the better to look at the group. 'Whom is
he speaking to in that charming, gentlemanly
manner?'

'I cannot see clearly, but to Heriot, I
should fancy, by that graceful allusion to the
boy's French bringing up. Yes, it is. I hear
Heriot's shrill voice in reply, and the strong
foreign accent which always crops up when
he's excited.'

'That Travers is just the sort of fellow
who would bully and swagger where he
thought he could do so unchecked.'

'He had better not try on such practices
with Heriot,' said Cleethorpe. 'That young
man has, I fancy, a spirit of his own. At all
events, if he takes after his father, he would
be one of the last to stand any— By Jove,
they are at it again.'

As he spoke, the little knot of men had formed again in the same place, and again Travers's voice was heard above the others, crying out, this time in louder and more passionate accents, 'Keep back, sir, will you? You have spoiled my stroke again. That time I believe you did it on purpose.'

'I didn't,' in Heriot's shrill accents.

'You did.'

'You're a liar!'

And immediately on the utterance of the words, there followed a dull heavy sound like a thud.

Travers had hit out, and caught Heriot on the cheek. Then with something that was more of a scream than an ordinary exclamation, Heriot was rushing in upon his adversary, when the bystanders laid hold of him, and Captain Cleethorpe rushing up, pushed his way through the crowd, and taking the lad by the arm, cried out, 'Mr. Heriot, what is the meaning of all this?'

The boy, who was trembling with excitement from head to foot, stared at him vacantly for a moment, then said, incoherently, 'He—I—' and then, to Cleethorpe's intense dismay, burst into a flood of passionate tears.

CHAPTER III.

EVERY morning at six o'clock, the bell in the turret of the stables attached to Lacklands, the pretty villa in the neighbourhood of Cheeseborough, where Lieutenant - Colonel Goole resides, is rung for full five minutes, its shrill notes warning all those who hear it, and who are in the Colonel's employ, that for them the new day has begun, and that they may at any time expect a visit from their master.

Mr. Boulger, who lives at Valparaiso Villa, the property adjoining Lacklands, and who made his money as a shipping agent at Birkenhead, objects very strongly to this bell, as do other residents in the neighbourhood. Colonel Goole receives their protests, which are sometimes made verbally, sometimes in writing, very politely, and in reply informs them, in a gentleman-like manner, and well-chosen terms. that he finds it necessary to make some such public announcement to the people employed by him, and that as an old Indian officer, accustomed to early rising, he considers the time he has fixed upon as the very latest at which work ought to be commenced. He himself, he avers, is always out of bed an hour before that time; and he might have added, is generally on the spot to see that the warning of the bell is not without its proper attention.

This morning, for instance, he has been through the stables, and looked over the occupant of each of his four stalls, has talked with the gardener about the coming fruit crop, and consulted the shepherd as to the chances of fine weather; and now, just as the clock is striking seven, is striding about with a spud in his hand, devising certain alterations in the little slips of garden specially set aside for the behoof of his children.

The sunlight is even now sufficiently strong to dazzle his eyes as he looks up from the ground which he has been marking out, and he is compelled to shade them with his hand before he can make out the figure of a man, mounted on horseback, slowly approaching up the valley. Colonel Goole's eyesight had stood him in good stead on many occasions in India, and is good still. 'Cleethorpe,' he says to himself, after his survey; 'Cleethorpe, on that leggy mare which he tried to make a charger of, but which he is quite wise in keeping for a hack. What can bring him here so early this morning? He's not a man to come out merely for the sake of a ride, or for breakfast; there must be something the matter in the regiment, I expect.' And without relinquishing his hold of the spud, Colonel Goole started off down the hill to meet his brother officer.

The Colonel's apprehensions were by no means set at rest by the Captain's manner or appearance. Both, however, were practical men, unaccustomed to beat about the bush,

or to attempt to mystify each other, and they
came to the point at once.

'Good-morning, Cleethorpe,' said the Colonel, when he was within earshot of his friend;
'what brings you out here so early this
morning? Something has happened, I suppose?'

'You're right, sir,' said Captain Cleethorpe,
returning his salute, ' something has happened.'

' Unpleasant?'

'Very unpleasant!'

'I thought so,' said the Colonel, who had
paused until his friend joined him, and who
now turned round and walked by the horse's
side. ' Please state shortly what it is.'

'A row in the billiard-room of the George,
last night.'

The Colonel's face darkened at these
words, and he muttered, 'Creditable that, by
Jove! Any civilian mixed up in it?'

'No, sir; the quarrel was between Mr.
Travers and Mr. Heriot.'

' George Heriot!' replied the Colonel

quickly; then shaking his head, 'I'm sorry for that. Go on.'

'Mr. Travers several times accused Mr. Heriot of unduly pressing upon him, and spoiling his stroke in the game that was being played. At length, in the most marked and offensive manner, he accused Mr. Heriot of having pushed his arm.'

'Well, Cleethorpe, well?'

'I regret to say, sir, that upon this provocation Mr. Heriot gave Mr. Travers the lie, and that then Mr. Travers struck Mr. Heriot a blow.'

'A blow! struck George a blow?' said the Colonel, stopping short, and looking up in horror at his friend. 'By Jove, Cleethorpe, I am not a rich man, but I would have given five hundred pounds sooner than this should have happened. Who were present at this scene?'

'Many, sir; quite a crowd. Captain Norman and I, some dozen of the regiment, and several townspeople. One of the waiters and the marker were in the room, too, at the time; in fact. as you will see from the sequel, it is impossible to hush the matter up.'

'Sequel! What, have you more to tell me?'

'I have, indeed, and the worst part of it.'

'By Jove, Cleethorpe,' said the Colonel, who had fallen into deep thought, 'Lord Oke-hampton will be furious when he hears of this; and if there's a meeting between these young men—'

'You may spare yourself the trouble of calculating the consequences of such a result, Colonel Goole; there will be no meeting.'

'No meeting; that's by your manage-ment then, Cleethorpe,' said the Colonel, lay-ing his hand on the Captain's arm; 'mutual retractations and apologies, eh? Cleverly managed, my friend.'

'I don't deserve your compliment, and I regret that you have quite misapprehended the state of affairs. Mr. Travers distinctly refuses to retract anything that he has said, or to apologise for the blow given to Mr. Heriot.'

'The deuce he does!' said the Colonel anxiously. 'Well, then, Cleethorpe, the days of duelling are over, and rightly, too, I suppose, but—but a blow is a deuced awkward thing; George Heriot can't sit down under that; he must have him out, sir, he must have him out!'

'That course has already been suggested to Mr. Heriot,' said Captain Cleethorpe; 'not by me, I am too old to be mixed up in such matters, but by some gentlemen more of his own standing in the regiment; but Mr. Heriot won't fight.'

'What!' cried the Colonel, so loudly and suddenly as to frighten Cleethorpe's horse; 'won't fight?'

'He declines to ask Mr. Travers for satisfaction for the insult passed upon him. The young man is a favourite in the regiment, and his comrades hesitated before accepting his reply. It was pointed out to him that the insult offered to him was the grossest which could be passed upon any gentleman, and one which it was impossible for him to bear, and remain in the society of gentlemen. Mr. Heriot did not attempt to argue the point; he simply declined to send a challenge.'

'But didn't he give any reason for this extraordinary conduct?'

'Not the least in the world. He said he had a reason which satisfied himself, but which he could not explain.'

'This is very bad, Cleethorpe.'

'Very bad indeed, Colonel. As I have told you, I thought it better to keep clear of the affair last night; but this morning I went to the young man's room—I knew something of his father in India, as I told you—and tried to represent to him the position in which he had placed himself. It was of no use. He still refuses to take proper notice of Mr. Travers's blow.'

'He must go, Cleethorpe,' said the Colonel, looking up at him.

'Not a doubt of that, Colonel. The prestige of the regiment would be ruined if he were suffered to remain. Two or three men expressed that opinion to me last night, amongst them Norman, who is quiet and sensible, and by no means hot-headed. Indeed, I feel it myself.'

'So do I,' said Colonel Goole quietly. 'You mentioned his father just now; I don't know how I shall be able to break it to Sir Geoffry, and he intended to make a soldier of the lad.'

'Ah!' said Captain Cleethorpe, patting his horse's neck, 'it was only last evening that I was half inclined to deplore my bachelor state, and to wish that I had a boy like his; but now I cannot be too thankful for the immense amount of anxiety and possible misery that I have been spared.'

'You're right. God help poor Sir Geoffry! He will suffer frightfully. I must write to him, of course, and to Lord Okehampton; and that will be a very pleasant business for me, by the way, for it was principally on my representation that Okehampton gave the boy his commission. However, we will go in and get our breakfast now, and afterwards I will

write the letters, and you shall take them in
with you and dispatch them. Hard lines for
Heriot—frightful hard lines for a man at the
close of an honourable career to find his hopes
blighted and his name slurred, and that by
no fault of his own. By the way, does the
young man know that he must go? He had
better apply for leave until the matter can be
formally arranged.'

'I settled that with him this morning, and
am the bearer of his application. He knows,
too, that he must give up all chance of entering the army.'

'How does he behave about that?'

'Very quietly, and not without a certain
amount of dignity. In spite of all that has
happened, there is something about the young
man's manner which one could never find in
a coward. If one could only know his reason
for this conduct!'

'That, you say, he distinctly refuses to
give?' said the Colonel.

'Most decidedly.'

'Then,' said the Colonel, shrugging his

shoulders, 'we can only act on what is brought
before us.'

'I suppose so,' said Captain Cleethorpe,
repeating the shrug, and turning his horse's
head in the direction of the stables, while the
Colonel moved towards the house.

Their talk at breakfast was about other
matters, and when the meal was finished, they
adjourned to the little study, and there, after
much cogitation and many alterations, their
joint labours produced the following letter:

> '*Cheeseborough, May* 18, 1860.

'My dear Heriot,—I much regret to be
compelled to announce to you some ill news,
which I fear will affect you very deeply. Like
most old soldiers, I am not a very good hand
with the pen, but you will understand that it
is not for any want of sympathy that I come
at once to the point, and tell you that your
son must send in his resignation of the commission which he holds in the Cheddar Yeomanry. It appears that last night he and
another subaltern, a Mr. Travers, came to

high words in a billiard-room in this town.
Your son gave Mr. Travers the lie, and Travers retorted by a blow. I need not point
out to you that after this, more especially as
the affair took place in public, and in the presence of several of the townspeople, there was
but one course to pursue. That course, however, Mr. Heriot, although it has been plainly
pointed out to him, declines to take, and is
content, as it seems, to sit down patiently
under the insult that he has received. Of
course, his continuance in the regiment under
these circumstances is impossible, as henceforward all fellowship with his brother officers, or respect from the men, would be at
an end.

'I cannot tell you, my dear Heriot, knowing as I do your acute sense of honour, how
deeply I sympathise with you under these
unhappy circumstances; more especially as I
am sure, if George had only done what might
have been expected of him, the matter could
have been easily arranged. This Mr. Travers
with whom he quarrelled is an underbred

bully, and from what I have heard from Captain Cleethorpe, who was present at the row, and whom I think you know, I could easily have prevented matters from going to extremities. George's refusal to notice the insult has, however, completely taken the matter out of my hands. He says he has a reason for his conduct, which is quite sufficient for himself, but declines to impart it to any of us. He is prepared to send in his resignation, and I have no option but to advise its acceptance. I write to Lord Okehampton accordingly by this post. Again assuring you of my deep regret, I am, my dear Heriot, sincerely yours,   MARKHAM GOOLE.'

'There,' said Colonel Goole, folding up the letter, 'this affair will either break the old man's heart, or cause him to break his son's spirit.'

'Do you think so?' said Captain Cleethorpe doubtfully; 'for my part, I look upon the first process as difficult, the last as impossible.'

CHAPTER IV

SENTENCED.

'GLAD you have come in, Mr. Riley; the General has rung twice.'

'And why didn't you answer the bell?' asked Mr. Riley, a tall, weather-beaten, gray-haired man, of soldierly appearance.

'No, I thank you,' replied the butler; 'when I have known him as long as you, perhaps I will, but our acquaintance is much too short at present; "and never let me see you before lunch time," he says to me the other day, and I made up my mind that I would act accordingly.'

'The General's rather short tempered in the morning,' said Riley, with a grim smile as he left the room to answer the bell, which pealed out for the third time.

'Short tempered,' said the butler to the

footman, who entered the pantry at the moment, bearing a tray of glasses; 'short tempered! He thinks he's among the niggers
still, I suppose, but he'll have to alter all that
now he's come over here.'

'Of course he will, Mr. Johnson,' said the
footman; 'I don't hold with blacks, which
is good enough to sweep crossings and sell
tracts, but not figures enough for indoor service.'

Meanwhile, Riley rapidly made his way to
the library, opened the door, closed it carefully behind him, and stood upright at the
attitude of attention, waiting for his master
to address him. The room was empty at the
moment, but through a doorway at the farther end of it came a man with quick, hasty
footsteps, bearing two letters in his hand. A
man above the middle height, and considerably past middle age, thin almost to gaunt-
ness, upright in his carriage, rapid and nervous in his movements. His iron-gray hair,
worn without parting or division, curled in a
thick crisp mass on his head. His small gray

moustache shaded his thin lips, but his cheeks
were whiskerless, and no beard softened the
outlines of the strong and heavy jaw, which
plainly indicated the owner's possession of a
quality characterised by his friends as firm-
ness, by his foes as obstinacy.

Such outward appearance had Major-General Sir Geoffry Heriot. As he entered the
room, he looked somewhat vacantly at the
servant, then seating himself at his writing-
table, spread his letters open before him, and
commenced the perusal of one of them. Riley
waited until his master again looked up, when
he said,

'You rang, General?'

Sir Geoffry roused in an instant.

'Three times, Riley. Where were you?'

'Gone to the stables, General, to look at
the horse that came last night. It's against
your orders for any of the servants to come
to you in the morning, and I thought you
would like to hear news of the horse. He'll
make a fine charger, General, and will carry
Mr. George splendidly.'

'How can you tell that?' said Sir Geoffry quickly; 'you never saw Mr. George!'

'No, General, that's true,' said Riley; 'but—'

'You never will see him,' said Sir Geoffry.

'Never see Mr. George,' cried the man in astonishment; 'why I thought in a month's time he was coming here?'

'Mr. George Heriot will never come here,' said Sir Geoffry, looking up sternly at his servant; 'more than that, there is no such person.'

'No such person as your honour's son?' cried Riley, who, like most of his countrymen, when excited flavoured his sentences with a vast amount of brogue.

'I have no son, Riley.'

'Is Mr. George dead?' asked the man, dropping his voice.

'He's dead to me,' said Sir Geoffry, in the same tone; 'do you understand?'

'That's just what I don't do,' said he, looking up in despair.

'All that you have occasion to know,' said

Sir Geoffry Heriot coldly, 'and you should not know even so much, if you had not served me faithfully so many years, is this: that the person whom I have hitherto been accustomed to think of as my son, and to whose companionship and affection I have been looking forward as the solace of my life, has done something which renders it necessary for me not merely to discard and disown him, but to forget that he ever existed.'

'Your honour,' said Riley, involuntarily taking a step nearer to his master, and speaking with trembling lips and outstretched hands, 'to discard and disown — is it Mr. George, your son?'

'Have I any other son, that you need ask?' said Sir Geoffry, unmoved. 'Understand, too, that henceforward his name will never pass my lips, and must never be mentioned by you. I am aware, Riley, that silence is one of your qualities, but have you ever spoken of my son's expected visit here to any of your new associates in the servants' hall?'

'Never, Sir Geoffry.'

'Never even mentioned his existence?'

'Never, General. Mr. George's name has never crossed my lips save to your honour, since we left the regiment.'

'That's right; now attend to me. I expect a visitor to-day. You will have timely notice of his approach, by seeing the carriage coming up the avenue, and you will take care to be in the way to open the hall-door. Mind that this is done by you, and none of the other servants; let them know, if they ask anything about it, that it is by my special orders. You will not ask the gentleman his name; if he gives it, you will keep it to yourself, and not even repeat it to me. You will simply announce him as a gentleman, send the carriage to the stables, and bid the driver come round again in half an hour's time. When I ring the bell you will see the gentleman to the door, and show him out, without a word. You understand me, without a word.'

'I understand, General,' said the man, with his head bent down, and in a low tone of voice.

'Now go!' and Sir Geoffry pointed to the door.

'It's Mr. George,' thought Riley to himself, as he went slowly down the passage; 'it's Mr. George! He's coming to see his father for the last time, and not all the angels in heaven, or all the other things anywhere else, would make the General budge an inch when he has made his mind up to do even so cruel a thing as this.'

When Sir Geoffry was left to himself, he took up the longer of the two letters which lay before him, and read it again attentively. As he read, the blood flushed in his bronzed cheeks, his teeth were set firmly together behind his thin lips, his eyes kindled, and at length crushing the letter in his hand, he began pacing the room with hasty strides.

'A coward!' he muttered, in short, broken sentences: 'a coward, that is it, neither more nor less. To think, after all I have gone through and all I have anticipated, that I should come back to this; that flesh and blood of mine should receive a blow, and, as Goole

phrases it, " sit down patiently under the insult." A coward, eh? Gave this other man
the lie, and when he hit out, naturally enough
—what else could have been expected of him?
—refused to call him out, but sits down patiently under the insult. That's the tailor's
blood cropping up in that—you can never get
rid of the taint; like gout it will skip one
generation, but it comes out in the next; it
passed by me and shows itself in him. Just
like your low-bred cur, who will fly out and
bark and growl, but runs away directly a stick
is shaken at him. To think that he should
have received a blow, and—What does Goole
say?' Here he referred to the letter. ' " Townspeople present." I am thankful to Provi-
dence that I did not obey my first impulse,
and go up to Cheeseborough to see this lad
and his regiment directly I landed. With the
exception of Goole and this man—what is his
name?—Cleethorpe—whom he refers to, they
know nothing of me except my name, and
they are not likely to remember that for long
after their drill meeting is over. They were

all county men, I recollect Goole telling me,
and Cheddar is a long way off, and has not
much communication with London, so that I
am not likely to be brought across any of
them. " This reason for his refusal to fight,"'
continued Sir Geoffry, again referring to the
letter, ' " this reason he declines to impart to
anybody." Declines to impart! What does
Goole mean by writing such stuff as that to
me, even if he be taken in by it himself?
Reason—a man has no reason for being a
coward save that he is one. And here I am,
with this word "coward" ringing out in every
sentence, and knowing that it is applied to my
own son !'

He stopped suddenly, and threw up his
arms in the violence of his rage and grief,
then let them drop by his side, and continued
mechanically pacing to and fro with his chin
resting on his breast.

After about an hour had passed away in
this manner, Sir Geoffry's quick ear caught
the sound of footsteps in the passage close to
the door. He had only time to throw him-

self into a chair at the writing-table, and to assume the appearance of being engaged with his pen, when the door was opened, and Riley appeared. Close behind him Sir Geoffry saw the outline of another figure, and it required all the self-command he possessed to subdue the nervous shivering, which ran through him at the sight from head to heel.

Riley studiously averted his eyes from his master as he made the announcement: 'A gentleman, Sir Geoffry!' Sir Geoffry replied, 'Show him in;' but, after the first glance, did not look up from the writing in front of him until he heard the sound made by the closing door. Then he raised his head, and rose from his chair, but as his glance fell upon the young man standing before him, his thoughts leaped back over the abyss of twenty years, and a woman's face, which he had not seen during that period, but which, when he last looked at it, bore just the same strange, proud expression, rose before his fancy. He sank back in his chair again, and shut the vision out with his hand.

'Father,' cried the young man, stepping forward.

In an instant Sir Geoffry was himself again.

'Son,' he replied, rising to his feet, and putting forth his hand to check the young man's advance, 'this is the first time we have ever interchanged these terms, and it will be the last.'

'Father!' again cried the youth.

'I am Sir Geoffry Heriot, if you please, to you as well as to everybody else. Whom you are now I know, but what you may be for the future is for your own decision, and utterly without any reference to me.'

The young man looked up as though doubting the evidence of his ears.

Presently he said:

'You have had a letter from me, sir?'

'I have had a letter from Colonel Goole, stating what occurred on Thursday night in a billiard-room at Cheeseborough,' said Sir Geoffry.

'But from me, I ask,' said the young man impetuously; 'had you not a letter from me, stating that I was coming to you forthwith, and that I would explain that occurrence?'

'I had,' said Sir Geoffry quietly; 'but there was no occasion for you to have troubled yourself to have come on such an errand. I have no doubt Colonel Goole states the circumstances correctly; you can take his letter and judge for yourself.' And he threw the letter across the table.

George Heriot took up the letter and read it through, Sir Geoffry watching him intently, muttering as he did so, 'And he can read of his own disgrace without turning a hair!'

'The facts are correctly stated, sir,' said George, folding the letter, and handing it back to his father.

.'Of course,' said Sir Geoffry, contemptuously; 'gentlemen are no more in the habit of perverting facts than of submitting tamely to insult. We will go through the statements seriatim if you please. You and this Mr. Travers,' said the General, referring to the letter, 'had this quarrel at a billiard-table?'

'We had.'

'He accused you of obtruding on his stroke, and of purposely pushing his arm?'

'He did.'

'You gave him the lie?'

'Yes.'

'And he then struck you a blow?'

'He did.'

'That blow you have not attempted to avenge. You remain, as it were, with a red mark of his buffet on your cheek. You have not demanded satisfaction for this insult that has been put upon you?'

'I have not.'

'On the contrary, you have refused to call this man to account?'

'I have.'

'And you dare, sir, to come here and confront me with such a decision as that in your mouth?' cried the General, almost shrieking with rage.

'I dare,' said George Heriot, very quietly.

His son's coolness had a subduing effect upon the elder man. His look was still disdainful, and his manner imperious, but his voice was considerably moderated as he said :

' Your daring to do so proves more plainly than anything else that we have never met before, and that you have been brought up in complete ignorance of my character.'

' I certainly was not brought up to regard you either as an idol whom I was to worship, or as a bully from whom I was to run away,' said the young man, still very quietly.

Sir Geoffry's face darkened, and he seemed as though about to again give vent to his passion. But he checked himself, and said :

' I am indebted to those to whom your early days were confided for having failed to represent me in the last objectionable character. As to the former,' he added grimly, ' they were not likely to make any mistake about that. However, that is not relevant to the subject at present under discussion. You allow that all that is said by Colonel Goole in this matter is true?'

' Perfectly true.'

' Then it only remains with me to an-

nounce the determination which I have come
to in the matter. Stay, though. Colonel
Goole tells me that you describe yourself as
having some reason for refusing to demand
satisfaction of this man.'

' Of any man,' interrupted George.

' Of any man,' repeated the General. ' I
beg your pardon, and accept your correction
in its wider sense. This reason you declined
to state to Colonel Goole, or to any of your
brother officers. Does your objection to mention it apply equally to me?'

' It does not.'

' No! Then you can give me your reasons?'

' I can.'

' And will?'

' Certainly.'

' I confess I shall be curious to hear what
can have been your motive for sacrificing a
very promising career, almost before you had
entered upon it.'

' My sole motive for refusing to fight a
duel—that is the right way to put it, as, even

had I been challenged, I should have declined
the meeting—was, that I had sworn a solemn
oath never to engage in such an encounter.'

Sir Geoffry laughed aloud.

' The old story,' he cried, with a sneer;
' the coward's never-failing plea. So tender
of his word, so regardless of his honour.
And to whom, pray, and under what circumstances, was this oath given?'

' To whom? To your wife: my mother.'

Sir Geoffry started, and shook himself as
though he had received a cut from a whip.
He steadied himself quickly, and then, placing
his fingers upon the table, remained standing.

' And you ask under what circumstances,'
continued the lad. ' I will tell you. The
first time I can recollect any allusion to it
was when I was quite a little child. We
were living then at Saumer, a little village
within a short distance of Boulogne. We
used to go into Boulogne in a kind of omnibus, drawn by one horse, and driven by a
man named Joseph. It used to start very
early in the morning, that the countrywomen

might be betimes at market with their fruit,
and flowers, and vegetables. And one morning, just as we were skirting the sands, we
saw a little knot of men gathered round something which they were slowly carrying away.
Joseph stopped his horse, and ran to see
what it was, and coming back told us that it
was the body of an officer who had been just
killed in a duel. That night I spoke to my
mother about it, and asked her what a duel
meant, and why the officer had been killed.
After she had explained this, she cried a
great deal, I recollect, and made me promise
never to allow myself to be mixed up in such
matters. The subject was never alluded to
again between us until'—and here the lad's
voice broke a little—'until she was dying.
We had had a long, long talk, and she had
told me of all that she wished me to do. I
was sitting by her; her eyes were closed, and
I thought she was sleeping, when she suddenly roused up, and clutching me by the
arm, reminded me of the scene which we had
witnessed from the Saumer omnibus, and of

the promise which I then made. "You were very young then," she said, "and you are but a mere child now, but you will have sense enough to understand me, and to do what I bid you, when I tell you that it is my urgent wish, and that I am going away from you, and you will never see me again. Say after me these words: 'I swear by my hopes of salvation, and by the love I have for my mother, that I will never fight a duel, or take part in one in any way.'" I repeated the words after her, then I laid down beside her, and she put her arms round my neck, and kept them there till she died.'

The boy ceased. The vivid recollection of what he had described had excited him somewhat as he proceeded, and his narrative had, he imagined, had some effect upon his father, who sat with his face averted, and his head resting on his hand.

But whatever emotion Sir Geoffry might have felt, he was careful to let no sign of it escape him. After a pause he looked up, and said, in hard, dry tones:

' It is a pity you did not think of all this
before you gave the lie to your brother officer, or that, having done so, you did not
suffer the fact to escape your memory. The
circumstances being as they are, I do not
allow for a moment that your statement is a
sufficient excuse for your conduct. But it
has had a certain effect. When I received
your Colonel's letter this morning, I determined upon disowning and discarding you on
account of your conduct as described to me
by him, without entering into any parley as
to the past or the future. That determination I adhere to, but in consequence of what
you have said, I feel it due to myself to let
you know something, at least, of the history
of the past. When you have heard it, you
will more readily comprehend your mother's
horror of duelling, and what may perhaps
have been a mystery to you—the reason that
the latter portion of her life was passed away
from me.

' Your grandfather was a tailor named
Causton, residing in a small hamlet near

London, where there was a good foundation
school. To this school he sent me, his son,
and there, when quite a child, I formed an
intimate friendship with a lad named Heriot.
This lad died when he was about eleven years
old, and his father, who was a clerk high up
in the India House, adopted me in his place,
on condition that I should bear his name, and
give myself up entirely to his direction. My
father was dead at that time, and I never cared
particularly about the tailor's connection, so
that I gladly accepted Mr. Heriot's offer, and,
under my new name, I was sent to Addis-
combe, and thence into the Indian army. I
stuck resolutely to my profession, never ask-
ing for leave of absence during twenty years.
Then I obtained a long furlough, and came
home to England. All traces of the Causton
name and the tailor parentage were obliterated
by this time. I was Major Heriot, well known
and highly respected throughout the Indian
service; and, as I had lived frugally, I had
been enabled to save ample means.

'I met your mother in society, and ad-

mired her immensely. She was one of two
sisters, both of whom were raved about; but
your mother's was the softer beauty of the
two, and in manner she was much the sweeter
and more innocent. My attentions pleased
her, my position was thought an eligible one
by her friends, and we were married. Within
a year of our marriage, and shortly after your
birth, your mother presented to me a gentleman named Yeldham, whom she had known
before she made my acquaintance. He was
an Englishman, but had lived most of his time
abroad, had foreign manners, and was accustomed to foreign ways. He was a dilettante
artist and an amateur musician, and was supposed to be particularly fascinating to women.
Your mother took great delight in his society,
and he was so much at our house that I spoke
to her about it. She laughed at the time, and
told me if I used my eyes I could see that it
was her sister, who was living with us, that
was in reality Mr. Yeldham's attraction. I
thought no more of it, and shortly after we
all went abroad, loitering up the Rhine to Ba-

den, where Mr. Yeldham joined us. I again
fancied I perceived an understanding between
your mother and this man, which was anything but agreeable to me. I spoke about it
in confidence to her sister, Miss Hastings,
and although she strove to make me believe
I was wrong, I was not satisfied with her explanation. Finally I watched their conduct at
a grand fancy ball given by a French banker,
who was staying at the place; and in consequence of what I saw, I sent Mr. Yeldham a
challenge. Twenty-four hours after that we
met at one of the small islands on the Rhine,
and I shot him through the chest. With his
dying breath he declared that I had been in
error throughout, and that it was not even
your mother with whom I had seen him at
the ball. He was a man of honour, and did
his best to save a woman's reputation, but of
course his statement was false.'

'What did my mother say?' interrupted
George.

'She corroborated Mr. Yeldham in every
particular, and accused me of being a mur-

derer,' said Sir Geoffry bitterly; 'and as we
held such very unpleasant opinions regarding
each other, I thought it best that we should
separate, and I accordingly returned to India.
Her horror of duelling, and the reason of my
separation from her, are now, I think, sufficiently explained.'

'Perfectly,' said George; 'but—'

'One moment,' interrupted Sir Geoffry;
'I have given you this explanation, which I
was by no means called upon to do; and I
now proceed to state to you my determination
with regard to yourself. You have disgraced
the name which I have raised, and for the first
time that I have borne it have caused me to
blush at its mention. The name is yours, and
I cannot forbid your bearing it; but you shall
never again be acknowledged or treated by
me as my son. From this moment I discard
and disown you. You are entitled, when of
age, to your mother's property; I am willing
to anticipate that event, and allow you to enjoy the income arising from it now, on condition that you assume another name, and

pledge your word never in any way to reveal
your identity, or claim relationship with me.'

'I am much obliged to you, sir,' said the
young man, struggling to repress his emotion,
'for your very generous offer, which does you
equal credit as a gentleman and as my father.
I will not touch one penny of my mother's
fortune until I am legally entitled to it. But,
meanwhile, you need have no fear of my degrading that name by which you set such
store, but which, after all, does not belong to
you.'

'Sir!' cried Sir Geoffry.

'Be good enough to hear me out,' said
George quietly. 'You cannot forget that you
are my father more readily than I will rid myself of every recollection that I am your son.
No intrusion of mine shall ever remind you of
my existence. I shall leave you to the enjoyment of the reflections which cannot fail to
arise when you look back upon your estimable
conduct, both as a husband and a father. But
I anticipate the pleasure of seeing you once
again. I shall make it the business of my life

to discover the real history of Mr. Yeldham's acquaintance with my mother; and when I find, as I am certain I shall find, that you were grievously deceived by your own vanity and jealousy, I shall have the pleasure of coming and proving it to you, as some slight return for your noble conduct towards my mother and myself. And now I must trouble you to ring the bell and order the carriage to be brought round.'

With this, and a slight bow, the young man turned on his heel and quitted the room.

For a moment Sir Geoffry was speechless; his rage choked him; then he said,

'What an insolent rascal! But, after all, it was better than whining; it shows he has some pluck left; and I was afraid he would whine.'

END OF THE PROLOGUE.

Book the First.

CHAPTER I.

MISS CAVE'S LODGINGS.

OUT of the bright and busy High-street of Wexeter, parallel with the narrow little court leading to the cathedral, there runs a small street of small houses, leading into an open space, and flanked on either side by a crescent. Big, heavy, old-fashioned red-brick houses, speaking of bygone times, when the gentry who have now established themselves in various country seats thought it no disgrace to dwell within the walls of the city, and when the peaceful and aristocratic quarter of South-Hedge, in which such as are left of them now

reside, was by no means sufficient to contain
them. At the present time, however, a different set of people is to be found in the
crescent, and an eruption of brass-plates has
broken out amongst its heavy railings. Doc-
tors are there, and even dentists, agents for
insurance companies, and solicitors; some of
the houses in the middle of the Eastern Crescent have been transformed into a chapel, and
one at the westernmost corner has only nar-
rowly escaped being converted into a shop.
The half-glazed door with the word 'office' on
its window-pane has prevented this degradation; but when you have passed this Rubicon,
you find yourself in a place furnished with a
counter, and shelves, and other appurtenances
of a shop, shoppy.

How the builders of the theatre ever ventured to select a site for that structure in such
a grave and decorous neighbourhood, it is difficult to imagine; but there it is at the other
end of the crescent, and, truth to tell, not very
far from the chapel. A square building, with
medallions of the tragic and comic muses let

into its front, and with an overhanging portico,
on one side of which is situated the box-office,
while on the other, during the daytime at least,
Miss Bult, the milliner, plies her trade. Whether the situation and the surroundings have
anything to do with it or not, it is impossible
to say; but it is a fact, that the theatre at
Wexeter always has stood high, not merely
in the opinion of those engaged in it, which
is of common occurrence enough, but in the
estimation of those who dwelt around it, and
on whose patronage it was greatly dependent.
Great actors have been bred and educated on
the circuit of which Wexeter was the principal
town. The management of this circuit has
been in one family for several generations, be-
queathed from sire to son, and has always been
carried on after the same regular respectable
fashion. These facts were of course known to
the townspeople and the neighbourhood; but
no stranger, wanting to engage a seat, could
possibly have walked into the box-office, without being at once convinced of the respectability of the entire concern.

For in the box-office, with the box plan spread out before her, while she occupied herself either with knitting or Berlin-work, or some humbler employment for her needle, sat Miss Cave during the whole of the day, looking, with her silver-rimmed spectacles, her pepper-and-salt 'front,' consisting of two large flat curls over each eye, and an impossible parting in the middle, her neat cap, and her muslin kerchief crossed over her shoulders, the embodiment of respectability. There in the box-office she sat, as a guarantee for the style of entertainment for which she would sell you a seat. No one with such an appearance could have any connection with burlesques, breakdowns, or comic singing. The 'Highland Fling, in character, by Miss M'Alpine;' the 'One-horse Shay,' by special desire, on the occasion of his benefit, by the low comedian; or a variety of singing and dancing between the pieces when the bill was short, might be looked for; otherwise Shakespeare or Sheridan, with a staid old-fashioned farce, formed the staple of the entertainment.

Miss Cave was an elderly lady—so old that none of the inhabitants of Wexeter had ever recollected her as anything else. Tradition reported that her father had been in the choir, and had been specially noticed for his fine voice by George the Third, when that old monarch and Queen Charlotte paid their visit to the city. And it is certain that Miss Cave always maintained amicable relations with the authorities of the cathedral, attending divine service regularly every Sunday, and never meeting canons, deans, or even the bishop himself, without receiving a pleasant greeting and a few words of salutation. Indeed, on the occasion of Miss Cave's annual benefit, a large number of the resident clergy not merely sent their families, but were themselves to be found seated in the dress-boxes of the theatre. The entertainment then provided never varied, commencing with one of Shakespeare's tragedies, concluding either with the *Critic* or the *Trip to Scarborough*. Miss M'Alpine knew that at such a time it would be useless for her to attempt to interpolate the

Highland fling, and the low comedian perfectly understood that he would not be called upon to exercise his vocal powers.

Miss Cave lives in a bright little house, one of the row just beyond the theatre—a little house just high enough for its top windows to look over the old red-brick wall of the deanery garden. With Miss Cave lived her brother Samuel, who had been for years unnumbered the recognised barber and perruquier of the theatre, and the temporary attendant on such of those great actors visiting it as did not bring their own servants. It was Mr. Samuel's boast that he had 'wigged and painted' more 'stars' than any other man out of London; but that he was getting a little tired of it now—a statement which, considering that most of his anecdotes were personal reminiscences of the elder Kean and his compeers, might—as regards the latter portion of it at all events—be deemed veracious.

The brother and sister occupy the parlours and the attics of the little house; the drawing-room floor is generally let as lodg-

ings, either to the permanent members of the
theatrical company, or to any distinguished
artist engaged as a temporary attraction. At
the present time they are occupied by a
leading lady of the company, Miss Pierrepoint, and her younger sister. Miss Cave has
the highest opinion of Miss Pierrepoint, not
merely professionally, but privately. The old
lady admires her lodger's appearance, voice,
manner, and style of elocution, thinks she is
a credit to the company, which has sent up
some of the first leading ladies to the metro-
polis, and is only anxious lest any London
theatrical manager should get a hint of the
hidden treasure and come down to bear her
away. But, above all, she admires Miss
Pierrepoint's modesty, and the propriety of
her private life. Some of Miss Cave's former
lodgers had been given to 'gallivanting' and
'carryings - on' — proceedings never explained
by the old lady in other terms, but generally
believed by her intimates to be in relation to
the other sex, and too horrible to mention.
Miss Pierrepoint is given to none of these

atrocities : she has very few visitors ; none, indeed, beyond Mr. Dobson the manager, Mr. Potts the prompter, and young Mr. Gerald Hardinge the scene-painter. She never goes out to supper, has no anonymous letters or flowers left for her, but spends all her time in working at her profession and finishing the education of her sister Rose.

Not that Miss Pierrepoint might not have had admirers in plenty, bless you; Miss Cave knows that. Gentlemen are constantly inquiring at the box-office who she is, and where she comes from; and the admiration evoked by her powers of acting is by no means confined to applause, but forms the topic of much conversation between the acts, as Miss Cave, hidden away in the little pay-box on the top of the landing, can hear very well through the pigeon-hole in front of her, where she takes the money and gives the change. The old lady has heard, too, that when Miss Pierrepoint went to the party at Mrs. Probus's—Probus was a carriage-builder and a Shakespearian enthusiast—she was made more

of than any other woman in the room, which
naturally accounted for her never having been
asked again. But 'nothing came of it,' the
old lady used to say, although she had expected that, on the night after Probus's party,
all the eligible young men of the town would
have called at No. 9 The Precinct, prepared
to lay their hands and fortunes at Miss Pierrepoint's feet.

No; there was no one actually in love
with her that Miss Cave could point to, unless it was Mr. Gerald Hardinge, the scene-
painter, who was a mere boy, much too young
for her. As the old lady remarked, she did
not hold with making a great outcry about
disparagement (by which she probably meant
disparity) of years; but Miss Pierrepoint must
be at least six years older than Mr. Hardinge; and there were temptations enough for
a man in the profession, without his having
a wife so much his senior. And he was a
deal too handsome, Mr. Hardinge was, to be
exposed to temptations of any sort more than
could be helped, Miss Cave thought, 'having

one of those heads, my dear, which would look so well cut off just above the shoulders, and without any shirt-collar, on a medallion at the south end of the choir.' He was a kind-hearted lad too, Miss Cave allowed, and generous with his money, when he had any, and gave little Rose Pierrepoint lessons in drawing for nothing; and the elder sister was agreeable to him, and liked him very much, though the old lady 'did not think there was anything between them.'

It was a hot night, towards the end of June; the heat had been stifling and oppressive all day; and the windows of Miss Cave's lodgings were thrown wide open for the admittance of as much air as could be found. This was little enough; but such as it was it came laden with a thousand odours from the flowers in the deanery garden, rejoicing the heart of Rose Pierrepoint, the sole occupant of the room, who was seated at a table, drawing by the light of a shaded lamp, and who raised her head from time to time, and glanced now at the open window, then at the closed door. As far as could be seen of her in her sitting position, a girl slight and small in figure, with a small head, delicate features, and large dark eyes. Her age was about sixteen, and she looked even younger; and the manner in which she wore her hair, taken off her forehead, and kept back by a comb, rendered her appearance still more youthful. Her hands were thin and delicate, as was especially noticeable when from time to time she drummed them impatiently on the table before her; while the frequent expression of anxiety or irritability discomposed her otherwise handsome face.

At length she seemed as if she could bear her occupation no longer. She threw down the pencil and walked to the window. The whole sky was darkened by an enormous purple cloud, save on the horizon immediately opposite the window, where one fading streak of yellow light was reflected on the girl's face. Dazzled by this, after the darkness in which she had been sitting, the girl shaded her eyes with her hand, and, bending out of the window, looked down the street in the direction of the theatre. Instantly she drew back, and, crossing the room, resumed her seat at the table. She had hardly done so, taking up her pencil again, and becoming apparently engrossed in her work, when a light step was heard on the stairs. The door opened, and a young man entered the room. The girl looked up from her drawing in the direction of the door.

'Is that Mr. Hardinge?' she asked.

'It is,' was the reply.

The man who said these words was known to the small world in which he lived (and consequently must henceforth be known in these pages) as Gerald Hardinge; but when the reader saw him two years ago he was called George Heriot.

In those two years a considerable change had taken place in the young man's appearance. He was darker and stouter; his figure was more set; while the growth of a light curling brown beard had rendered him much more manly-looking. He was dressed in a light gray suit of clothes, much worn, and carried a soft felt hat in his hand.

'All alone, Rose?' was the first exclamation, in a tone of disappointment.

'Yes, Mr. Gerald,' said the girl quietly. 'Madge is not come back from the theatre.'

'The piece is over,' said Hardinge. 'I heard them ringing-in the orchestra for the last piece as I came away from the painting-room. What's the last piece to-night?'

'The *Warlock of the Glen*,' said the girl; 'and Madge don't play in the *Warlock*.'

'I should think not,' said Hardinge with a sneer.

'But she won't be home yet,' continued Rose. 'She told me she had something very particular to do, which would detain her perhaps for a couple of hours after she had finished. I was not to sit up for her if I was tired; and I was to tell you or Mr. Potts, if either of you came, that you were not to wait for her, as she would not be home till late.'

'All right,' said Hardinge, discontentedly enough; 'her commands must be obeyed.'

He was moving towards the door, when, thinking he had been somewhat ungracious, he turned back to the table, and, pointing to the drawing on which the girl had been engaged, said: 'At it still? What an industrious little woman it is! Let me look, Rose.' And he put out his hand, as though to take it.

But Rose threw a sheet of cartridge-paper over the sketch, saying, 'Not to-night, Mr. Hardinge; come to-morrow, and you shall see it.'

'Right,' he said; 'I will come to-morrow morning, and we will have another lesson. Good-night, little one. Tell your sister I called.' And he nodded and left the room.

When she heard the street-door close behind him the girl stole softly to the window, and watched his retreating figure down the street. When she could no longer distinguish it she turned sadly away.

'Was there ever any one so handsome? was there ever any one so fascinating?' she murmured to herself.

An hour afterwards, and the girl's mind

was still filled with visions of Gerald Hardinge, in her dream-haunted sleep; while Gerald Hardinge himself was pacing up and
down the street, with rage and jealousy at his
heart.

CHAPTER II.

THE streets of Wexeter, save during the period set apart for the militia training, or other times of festivity, are left solitary and deserted at a comparatively early period of the evening. The railway omnibuses, bound for the different hotels, roll from the great central station up the High-street at stated intervals up to ten o'clock; and about that hour small parties of pleasure-seekers may be seen here and there wending their way homeward from the theatre, or from the little social gatherings where they have spent an unmistakably quiet evening. But, by that time, such places as in the day are the busiest haunts of traffic—if any region within the limits of the dull and decorous old city can be so spoken of—have

relapsed into quiet, while in the precincts of
the cathedral, in the still aristocratic region
of South-Hedge, and in the straggling suburb
of villas which has grown up thereabouts, all
symptoms of life have died out at a much
earlier hour, and the entire neighbourhood
has long since been hushed into repose.

At half-past nine o'clock on the night when
Rose Pierrepoint, sitting over her drawing,
was interrupted by a visit from Gerald Hardinge, a tall woman issued from the stage-door
of the Wexeter Theatre, and was suddenly
confronted by Mr. Gonnop, the hall-keeper,
who was smoking a long clay pipe, and pa-
trolling the measured space of pavement outside, and to whom she wished 'good-night.'

'Good-night, Miss Pierrepoint,' responded
the hall-keeper; 'it looks amazing thick over
there,' he added, pointing with his pipe in
the direction where a large black cloud was
spreading over the city, 'and we'll have rain
before long, I reckon. Let's hope it'll come
down, miss, and get all clear again before next
Thursday.'

'And why particularly next Thursday, Gonnop?' asked Miss Pierrepoint, in a clear voice.

'Your benefit night, miss!' said the man, looking up at her in wonder; 'can't have forgotten that, surely?'

'I had, indeed, for the moment; but now I remember, and thank you for your good wishes.'

'Not that fine weather always does it,' said Gonnop, slowly emitting his smoke and looking steadily at her, 'being good for tea-gardens, and steamboat excursions, and ridiculous things of that sort, as is by their very nature contrary to theatres. For, look you, when the sun is shining — good-night,' said Gonnop, bringing his sentence to a hurried conclusion as the lady moved rapidly away.

When Miss Pierrepoint reached the end of the cul-de-sac in which the stage-door was situated, she turned to the right, and looking straight before her, could have seen Miss Cave's house, conspicuous by the brightness of its knocker and the shining cleanliness of

its door-step, within fifty yards. Their proximity to the theatre was indeed almost as great
a reason for the popularity of Miss Cave's
lodgings as their comfort and respectability;
but on this occasion Miss Pierrepoint had no
intention of proceeding direct to her resid-
ence; but after looking carefully round to see
that she was not followed or watched, she
turned off at an acute angle, and quickening
her footsteps speedily found herself in the
aristocratic quarter of South-Hedge.

The quarter before the hour chimed out
from the cathedral clock as she passed into
South-Hedge, where the lights were already
beginning to appear in the bedroom windows,
and where her footfall was the only sound
breaking the solemn silence. Past the newly-
built almshouses, whose gothic proportions,
which were the delight of the surrounding
gentry and the fashionable local architect,
stood dim, and black, and blurred against the
background of thick purple cloud behind them;
over the railway bridge, in the hollow beneath
which the huge engines destined to the ser-

vice of goods traffic, apparently undecided as to what was best for them to do, were called upon now to progress a little, now in an equal degree to retreat, and were ever and anon shrieking out their doleful lamentations at the indecision of their drivers.

Breasting the hill now, and now on the top of it in something like open country, villas scattered here and there, perched in grounds where the landscape gardener had sought to rival the handiwork of nature, and for the most part had signally failed; a brand-new stucco church, built in imitation of a celebrated prototype in stone, but looking pale and unhealthy, of the complexion of a slack-baked, ill-toasted muffin; then, very much out of place, a squat dumpy toll-gate, the sole remnant of the pre-suburban locality, of the pre-genteel day, when, teste the weather-beaten sign-post still extant, Manor Mead was known as Dumpington, and the almshouses and the villas, and the slack-baked church, had no existence.

The turnpike-gate was closed, and no light

was to be seen in the toll-house, as Miss
Pierrepoint, winding her way at the back of
it, turned into a narrow lane which was shaded
and screened by the high growing hedges on
either side. Here, after a hasty glance round
to assure herself that there was no one nigh,
she relaxed the swiftness of her pace and
threw back her veil, holding up her face to
catch whatever air might have found its way
into the quiet little retreat. Then she peered
long and anxiously into the darkness, and
turned her head towards the quarter from
whence she had come, as though listening for
approaching footsteps. But she heard nothing,
save the first dull long rumble of distant thunder which immediately preceded the striking
of the cathedral clock.

'Only just ten,' she said to herself. 'I am
here before my time then as usual, and, as
usual, he will be after his. What could have
brought him down here, I wonder, now? Not
that I need wonder, when I know well enough
that the want of money, and the idea that I can
be of use to him in some scheme for raising

it, are the only things now which induce Philip to break off, for ever so short a time, from the life which exercises such a fascination over him, and to come to me.'

She listened again, but after a minute resumed her pacing to and fro.

' I wonder if he ever thinks for a minute how and where it will all end? Whether, in the easy-going current of his life, the idea ever comes across him of the position I occupy, not merely by his tacit consent, but by his express desire? If he ever does think of it, he must be a very different man from the Philip Vane of two years ago, to allow it to continue, or to bear it calmly. Why, then the mere notion would— What a fool I am to trouble myself with such memories! Whatever may be the change in him, it cannot be greater than it is with me; and all I have to do is to accept the present state of things, and to make the best of it. This must be he at last!'

She turned swiftly round, as she caught sight of a man's figure coming round by the toll-house. The next minute a tall man joined her, and after a hasty glance around, put his arms round her, and bending down kissed her cheek.

'You need not have looked, Philip, to make sure that we were unobserved,' she said, with a short laugh. 'There was no one near to see you take the unwarrantable liberty of kissing your wife! You are generally prudent enough to select as our place of meeting some spot where there would be no chance of interruption.'

As he heard these words, and marked the tone in which they were spoken, a dark savage look crossed the man's face. It was gone in an instant, and his big black eyes were laughing merrily and his white teeth were gleaming brightly between his smiling lips, as he said:

'Savage to-night, old lady! Upset, eh, Madge? Don't like to be kept cooling her pretty heels in this particularly cut-throat-looking lane waiting for me, is that it?' And once again he placed his arms about her and kissed her cheek.

'No,' she said, 'that isn't it particularly. I don't know that I am savage, and I do know that I am accustomed to wait my lord's convenience.'

'Well, there, don't say any more about it,' the man said, in a sharper tone. 'I could not get away before, and that's enough. You got my telegram all right?'

'Of course, or I should not be here.'

'How confoundedly sharp you are to-night, Madge; down upon every word I say! Nothing gone wrong, has there? How's the booking for the benefit?'

'Very good, indeed; the house will be more than full, I think.'

'That's right, the money will just come in handy. I made rather a mess of it at Taunton yesterday.'

'Have there been races at Taunton?'

'Yes, of course; that's why I came on to see you. Shouldn't have been in the neighbourhood for some time to come, and therefore thought I had better take advantage of the chance.'

'Then it was really to see me that you came this time, Philip?' said the girl, nestling towards him, and looking up into his face.

'Of course it was, my dear!' he replied. 'What did you think it was—not business? There is no information to be got, no money to be made out of you?'

'Isn't there?' she said quietly; 'I thought there was.'

'You know what I mean,' he said. 'By the way, don't forget to send me that benefit money as soon as you get hold of it. You could send it to the club, you know. What do you think the figure is likely to be?'

'The figure?'

'Yes, the amount, the sum total. Heavens on earth, Madge, how slow you are!'

'Yes,' said the girl quietly; 'I am thoroughly provincial; you see I have not had the chance recently of having my wits sharpened, by contact with the clever people in London! You want to know the sum to be realised by the benefit? I should say forty-two or forty-three pounds.'

Philip Vane gave a low whistle.

'That's a very mild amount,' he said. 'I was looking for something much higher than that! By George, Madge, this will never do! Three pounds a-week, and a benefit producing under fifty pounds; those are starvation prices! I must take you up to London. I suppose you would do there, though it's a confounded pity you can't sing and dance!'

'Yes,' said the girl bitterly, 'those are qualifications, the absence of which, in his wife, every man ought to regret.'

He looked up at her under his eyebrows, but it was too dark for him to catch the expression of her face. There was, however, no mistaking the sneer conveyed in the tone of her voice. It was the second time during their short interview that she had thus offended him.

'What ails you to-night?' he said. 'What do you mean by sneering and gibing at me in this manner?'

'What do I mean!' she cried. 'I will tell you plainly what I mean—I mean that I am

sick of the manner in which you treat me!
You think that I am dull and stupid, but I
am neither so stupid nor so dull that I cannot
see plainly enough the value you put upon
me, without the necessity for your insulting
me by explaining it in words. I am your
wife, which means your drudge, your bread-
winner. Be it so; I don't repine, I did not
expect to be made a fine lady of, or to live
in idleness after you married me; but I did
expect that you would be content with me
and my talents, such as they were, and would
not complain while I worked my hardest, even
if my earnings might be small.'

She paused and stood confronting him,
her head erect, her hands nervously clasped
together beneath her cloak.

'Have you anything more to say?' he
asked in a low voice.

'Yes,' she continued. 'I want to know
when there is to be an end to this deception?
When you intend to acknowledge me openly
as your wife, and take me out of my present
position, which is inexpressibly painful to me,

and, mark my words, infinitely perilous to
you? I do not want rest, or ease, or luxury.
I did not expect what most women are led to
expect, that they are to look to their husbands for support: God knows, I am willing
to work, and not merely willing, but delighted. I do not know that I should be
happy without my work, but I want you to
give me my position as your wife, and to be
content with what I earn in that position.'

As she ceased speaking, the low rumble
of the thunder, this time much nearer, was
again audible. There was a pause for a moment as its last faint mutterings died away,
then Philip Vane said:

' You're right, Madge, in what you say,
and I was a brute to grumble, knowing how
hard and how cheerfully you work. And
you are right, too, about your position. It
is hard lines for you to have to come out
here to meet me on such a night as this is
going to be; to have to tramp all along the
road after playing—'

' It is not that, Philip,' interrupted the

girl. 'I don't mind that. I don't mind the hardship; all I hate is the deceit, the having to hide the fact of our marriage even from Rose, the having to nod and smile at the kindly prophecies of the old landlady at the lodgings as to my future, the having to receive attentions from honourable men, which would be naturally gratifying to an unmarried girl, which are degrading to me as your wife.'

'Yes,' said Philip Vane, 'I understand all that, of course, and as soon as I can I will put it right. I cannot do it just now, but I hope in a few months to make that all square. By the way, Madge, talking about attentions, what about the scene-painter—is he still here?'

'Yes, he is still with the company.'

'And still as spoony as ever?'

'I don't know about being 'spoony;' I think he is very fond of me, but he's a mere boy, you know, and—'

'Yes, I know! And have you still got that notion that you told me about his being a swell?'

'I have no doubt that he is a gentleman by position and education; beyond that I know nothing.'

'Exactly; that's quite enough! I shouldn't discourage his spooniness if I were you, Madge; something may turn up out of it. Don't you fear my being jealous. I can trust you, old woman; and if this man ever came into any money, or was received back by his friends, from whom you seem to suppose he has run away, we may make something out of him. He's written you some letters, I suppose?'

Madge hesitated for a moment.

'Yes, some,' she said.

'Ah! I don't want to see them, bless you,' cried Philip Vane; 'I can trust you perfectly, only I think you had better keep them, not tear them up or destroy them in any way; they may be useful one of these days. By Jove! here it comes,' he cried, as, after a few thick drops, a heavy peal of thunder broke right above their heads. 'We had better make a bolt of it at once. I've got a cab waiting the other side of the turnpike,

and can set you down where you like. Don't
be afraid, Madge; the driver doesn't know
me, and I'll take care he doesn't recognise
you.'

The storm was sharp while it lasted, but
was soon over. Miss Cave, who had sat up
for her lodger and 'gone round the house,'
as was her wont no matter how late the
hour, after every one else had retired to rest,
knocked at Miss Pierrepoint's door to inform
her that the clouds had quite cleared away,
and that the moon was shining brightly.

'A good omen for Thursday, my dear,'
added the old lady, as she retired to bed.

'I hope so,' said Madge to herself; 'I
hope so, for then Philip will get this money
that he says he wants. O, my God!' cried
the girl, as she seated herself on the edge of
the bed, 'how rapidly the romance is dying
out of my life! Never has he spoken so
plainly as to-night, never striven so little to
disguise himself! The money, and the money,
and the money! To take what I can earn
down here, to wish that I could earn more in

London, to bid me gull the boy and lead him on, and take care that I keep his letters, of which something might be made! All this Philip did not scruple to do, and then he pats my cheek and tells me " he trusts me"! '

About the same time Philip Vane, the sole occupant of the smoking-room at the Half Moon, was moodily puffing out the last fragment of his cigar.

' Forty pounds,' he muttered to himself, ' and I looked for at least seventy. Rode as rusty as a nail when I said I wished she could sing, and was cantankerous about everything! Worrying about her "position," too. I thought I had settled that question, but to-night she chose to revive it. I shall have to put my foot down upon one or two of these things, and upon Miss Madge herself if she doesn't mind.'

So saying, Philip Vane threw the stump of his cigar into the empty fireplace, and strode off to bed.

CHAPTER III.

Mr. Philip Vane was up early the next morning, intending to go off to town by the first express train, which left Wexeter soon after nine. He always travelled in first-class carriages and by express trains; always went to first-class hotels, asked for the best rooms, and lived on the most luxurious fare. He was one of those self-indulgent scoundrels who always found it necessary to make an excuse for the manner in which they pet and pamper themselves. Mr. Philip Vane had a stock of these excuses, which he had used so long and so frequently, that he actually began to believe in them. Thus, in regard to his travelling, he was in the habit of saying that time was money, that it was important for him to waste as little as possible of the day upon the road,

and that, travelling by express, he was enabled to transact business up to the last minute
at the town which he was leaving, and to be
ready to commence afresh the instant he arrived at his destination. Also, in regard to
his selection of the best hotels and his luxurious habits generally, he would remark that,
as he depended entirely upon his own exertions for his income, it was necessary that he
should keep himself in good condition, and
obviate as far as possible the ill effects of the
constant mental strain, by attention to his
bodily comforts.

Listening to this style of conversation, one
would have imagined that Mr. Vane was a
professional man in large practice, a busy merchant, or a gentleman holding in his own hands
the control of several large estates; instead o¹
being, as he was, a very common sharper, liv¯
ing on his wits. On those very rare occasions,
when he permitted any of his more intimate
associates to think that he was taking them
into his confidence, he would speak of himself
as ' a kind of modern Ishmael, sir; a sort of

fellow whose hand has been against every man,
and who, consequently, has had every man's
hand against him; but who has managed to
get on tolerably notwithstanding.'

Those assertions, like most others emanat-
ing from the same source, were wholly and
entirely false. Mr. Philip Vane's hand, instead of having been raised against every man,
had generally passed its time in patting the
shoulder, or gently insinuating itself under the
arm of every man from whom he thought he
could reap the smallest benefit. All things to
all men was Mr. Philip Vane: specious, sly,
frank, cunning, outspoken, reticent, just as
suited the occasion. This hazy comparison
of himself with Ishmael arose from the fact,
that he had never enjoyed the advantage of
parental rearing. His earliest recollections
were of the preparatory school in the suburbs
of London, where, smallest among the small
denizens of that little world—too small even
to be placed in the lowest class—he roamed
about the house and garden, and learned his
alphabet from some elder pupil inclined to

gratify his dignity by teaching him. There
he remained for some years, until old enough
to be removed to a grammar-school. Previous
to this removal, he, for the first time, experienced that greatest of all delights of a school-
boy, the charm of 'going home.'

Home, as realised by little Vane, was a
large house in a fashionable square in Brigh-
ton, belonging, as the child understood, to his
uncle, his father's brother, a leading physician
of the place. Doctor Vane Philip remembered
as a quiet little man, with white hair and a
thoughtful face, who used to pat the boy's
head, and surreptitiously give him half-crowns
—surreptitiously, that is to say, as far as concerned Mrs. Vane, a full-blown handsome woman, whom Philip always remembered with
flowers in her cap, and a very fresh complexion.
From the first, Philip had a dim childish notion that the doctor was afraid of Mrs. Vane,
whom, as the child learned in the course of
time, he had married when a widow, and who
had two sons, one with very large whiskers,
and the other with a black-and-white dog.

When the child came back for the next holidays, he learned that the dog-owning son had gone to Spain, which was a long way off, as he understood, to fight for something or somebody not clearly defined; but the other son with the whiskers was still there, and took Philip up to his bedroom, which was at the top of the house, and made him very sick by insisting upon his smoking a pipe—a proceeding which seemed fraught with great delight to the whiskered gentleman. When Philip came home six months afterwards, at Christmas, he found the house in sad tribulation, for the son with the dog was dead, and the son with the whiskers had gone to Australia, not, as the boy gathered from the talk among the servants and the visitors to the house, without having distinguished himself by squandering a vast amount of money and running very deeply into debt. The Doctor, Philip noticed, was thinner, whiter, and more thoughtful than ever; and though Mrs. Vane wore as many flowers in her cap, she seemed to have dropped suddenly into an old woman, and shed her

teeth, as he had heard of deer shedding their
horns, while her fresh complexion was, he noticed, muddled and streaky.

The boy never saw his uncle alive again;
he was sent home from school to attend the
funeral, and formed one of a very small pro-
cession which, in the roaring wind and drifting
rain, struggled up one of the back streets of
the town to the little Evangelical chapel, at
which, at his wife's command, the kindly old
Doctor had given regular attendance, and in
the burying-ground attached to which his remains were laid. After the ceremony, the
little funeral party broke up, the well-known
yellow carriage of the physician who had paid
the last respects to his old friend stood at the
churchyard-gate, ready to bear him off on his
round of visits ; an old school-friend of the
deceased, who had come down from town,
jumped into a cab to catch the return train ;
and Philip and the lawyer got into the mourn-
ing-coach to return together. On their way
back, the lawyer told the boy that Mrs. Vane
was not well enough to see him, but that he

was to go back to school that evening as soon
as he had had his dinner; then, to Philip's
great wonderment, asked him whether he had
read *Robinson Crusoe* and *Philip Quarll*, and
whether he did not think he should like to be
a great traveller like those heroes. The meaning of these questions was explained a few days
afterwards, when the schoolmaster called him
into the apartment which was alternately a
reception-room and a torture-chamber; and
instead of, as the boy expected, bidding him
prepare for immediate punishment, told him
that he was to leave school the next day for
Plymouth, where his passage had been taken in
one of the steamers immediately starting for the
West Indies, he having been bound apprentice
to a cousin of Mrs. Vane's, who was a merchant
and planter in the island of St. Vincent.

Philip Vane went to Plymouth, and to the
West Indies, but not to St. Vincent. Indeed,
he carefully avoided that island, having, while
on board the royal mail steamer Shannon,
made the acquaintance of several young gentlemen who were going out to join her Ma-

jesty's land forces. then quartered at Jamaica;
and by whose aid the lad, quick at games of
skill, and lucky at games of chance, turned the
fifty pounds with which he had been presented
by Mrs. Vane's agent on sailing into a sum
worth four times the original amount. For
two or three years he remained in the colonies,
enjoying the hospitality invariably extended
there to every one who makes himself agreeable, living at the different messes, riding races
for the officers, staying with the merchants at
their up-country villas, and providing himself
with pocket-money by bold and lucky card-
playing. By the time that the desire to return
to his native country became too strong to be
denied, Mr. Philip Vane had mixed so much
with the military, and was so thoroughly con-
versant with their manners and customs, that,
on his arrival in England, he deemed it expedient to announce himself as Captain Vane.
It was as Captain Vane. ostensibly fly-fishing
for his amusement at Chepstow, but in reality
hiding from the officers of the sheriff of Mon-
mouth, acting in conjunction with their bro.

ther-officers of Middlesex, that he made the acquaintance of Miss Pierrepoint, who at the time was acting in that ancient town. His intentions towards that young lady were at first strictly dishonourable; but finding that she was not to be won by anything short of the marriage ceremony, and believing that he saw in the development of her talent the foundation of a future income for himself, he honoured her by making her his wife. Captains becoming somewhat common, he gave himself a kind of billiard-room brevet, and appeared as Major Vane, under which title he was favourably known in a shady fifth-rate little club, composed of adventurers like himself, and their victims, calling itself by the high-sounding name of the Craven, and locating itself in a dingy little street in the neighbourhood of Piccadilly; had his presence 'remarked' by the reporters of sporting newspapers as a regular attendant at the principal turf-meetings, and led that odd sort of flashy, swindling, disreputable existence which has so many votaries in the present day. Though two years had

passed since his marriage, he had never introduced his wife to any one, and had insisted
upon her keeping their connection secret, even
from the little sister who was her sole relative.
From time to time he appeared at places where
she was acting, as he had just appeared at
Wexeter, giving her the benefit of his society
sometimes for a longer, sometimes for a shorter
period, but invariably insisting, whether present or not, on receiving two-thirds of the
salary which she earned by her exertions, and
leaving her and her sister to subsist on the
remainder.

Had the salary thus earned been tolerably
large, it is not improbable that Major Vane's
conjugal attentions might have been greater
than they actually were; but the Major con-
fessed to himself that his matrimonial speculation, as a speculation, had been a failure. In
confidential communication with himself, the
Major did not scruple to own that he had not
much regard for his wife. Even when he
perpetrated marriage, it was from the com-
mercial aspect that he regarded the step; and

from that point of view it had been a decided
failure. It ought to have turned out right;
he himself could check off a score of instances
in which worthy gentlemen, friends of his own,
were deriving large sums from the theatrical
earnings of ladies who were their acknowledged or unacknowledged partners; but these
ladies were spirited persons, with little cloth-
ing and less grammar, whose portraits were
in the photographers' windows, and whose
Christian names, affectionately diminished,
were in the mouths of London generally.

More than once he had suggested to his
wife that an equally glorious career lay before
her if she only chose to embrace the opportunity and accept an engagement which, without his connection with her being at all known,
he could procure for her; but she invariably
shook her head and refused, remaining at
Wexeter, or some such dreary place, 'doing
her spouting,' as he pleasantly but ironically
called it, for a salary of three pounds a week
and a benefit, which did not realise more than
forty pounds.

Major Vane, however, was a philosopher.
His marriage had been a mistake; he owned
it to himself, but to no one else. And by the
time that he had descended to the coffee-room
to breakfast on the morning after the meeting
in the lane behind the turnpike, he had thoroughly determined on ridding himself of the
connection at the first available opportunity.
Meantime, he should receive the money for
the benefit and the two-thirds of the week's
salary; and when an opportunity offered itself,
he should grasp it, and Miss Pierrepoint would
hear of him no more.

While the omnibus containing this large-
souled gentleman was moving towards the
railway station, Miss Pierrepoint emerged
from her lodging and made the best of her
way towards the theatre. It was very early for
a rehearsal, even at such an unconventional
theatre as that of Wexeter; but with a view
to see whether she could not make some effect
in other than merely 'spouting' parts, and
thus please her husband, Miss Pierrepoint had
determined on playing for her benefit the

part of Phœbe in *Paul Pry*, one of those wait-
ing-maids known only to the stage, who carry
their hands in the pockets of their little black-
silk aprons, who are the chosen recipients of
their young mistresses' secrets, and the terror
of the lives of the elderly gentlemen, their
masters. Phœbe has songs to sing, and the
leader of the band, who, like every other person in the theatre, would have done anything
for Miss Pierrepoint, was coming early to try
them over with her. Phœbe has a certain
amount of interchange of repartee with the
principal character; and the low comedian,
whose notion of repartee consisted in making
faces at the gallery, and whose ' dry humour,'
so often lauded, resolved itself into forgetting
his part, and substituting the slang sayings of
the day, was coming to ' go through their
scenes.' After that there was a full rehearsal
of *Romeo and Juliet*, which was to be the leading piece on the benefit evening; so that it
was tolerably late in the day before Miss
Pierrepoint's work was over.

Just as she was moving toward the stage-door, she felt her arm touched, and a low voice said in her ear:

'Won't you speak to me?'

Turning round she saw Gerald Hardinge; he was dressed in his working garb, a loose canvas jacket and trousers, spotted here and there with great daubs of paint.

'Mr. Hardinge!' she cried, putting out her hand.

'No,' he said, drawing back, 'I cannot shake hands with you now; I have been at work and have not had time to wash the traces of it off. I looked down from the "flies" and saw you were going away, so hurried down to stop you, as I have something to say to you.'

'I am very glad you did; I was sorry to have missed you last night—'

'Yes,' interrupted the young man, 'but we cannot talk here in this passage with the wind blowing in, and old Gonnop listening to every word. Come down on to the stage, there is no one there now, and we can have it all to ourselves.'

She turned back, and passing through the

littered mass of disused scenery stacked up
against the walls, they went down on to the
stage, now but very partially illumined by a
faint gleam of light, coming through the window at the back of the distant gallery. For
a minute neither of them spoke, then Miss
Pierrepoint said:

'What has kept you at work so late to-
day, Mr. Hardinge? I have heard of no new
piece in preparation.'

'No,' he said, 'there is nothing new, only
I think it would be a disgrace to the theatre
if we put on that worn and ragged old pair of
flats for the garden scene in *Romeo and Juliet*,
and I persuaded old Potts to let me touch it
up afresh.'

'Was it only for the credit of the theatre
that you did that?' asked Madge, looking softly
at him.

'Well, no, perhaps not,' he said. 'I daresay I should not have done it if it had been
Miss Delamere's benefit, or if Miss Montmorency had been playing Juliet. You know well
enough why I did it.'

'You are a kind, good boy, Gerald,' said Miss Pierrepoint, softly laying her hand on his arm, 'and never mind giving up your time, or taking trouble for me.'

'Kind, good boy, am I?' said he petulantly; 'it is very little I am able to do, but even that don't meet with much return.'

'Gerald!' said Miss Pierrepoint, 'what do you mean?'

'Where were you last night?' asked he, turning suddenly on her; 'where did you go to after you had finished here?'

'You have not the slightest right to ask me that question, Mr. Hardinge,' said Miss Pierrepoint, drawing herself up and looking straight at him, 'and certainly not to ask it in that tone.'

'I know I have no right,' interrupted Gerald.

'But as I have no reason to be ashamed of what I did,' continued Miss Pierrepoint, without heeding him, 'I do not mind telling you that I went to meet a person on important private business of my own.'

'And you did not get back until nearly midnight,' said Gerald.

'How do you know that?'

'How do I know it? Because I saw you return. I walked up and down the street in front of your door, from the time Rose told me you were out, until I saw you safe once more within the house.'

'What, were you there during all that terrible storm?' asked Miss Pierrepoint.

'Yes, I was. I did not mind that; there was far too great a storm going on within my breast for me to pay much attention to the thunder and lightning; I thought perhaps you had gone to meet some man, and I was nearly mad.'

'My poor boy,' said Madge soothingly.

'O, Madge, Madge! if you only knew what I suffer through jealousy; all this morning I have been like a lunatic, looking down on to the stage, and seeing that old Boodle make love to you at rehearsal.'

'But Mr. Boodle plays Romeo, Gerald!'

'Yes, I know all about that; of course he

must do it; and he is fifty years old, and wears a wig and false teeth, but still I hate to see him or any one else come near you, or touch you.'

' But why are you so jealous, Gerald?'

' Why? Because I love you. You know it, Madge, you know this, you are certain of it, and yet you ask me why I am jealous.'

' Yes, Gerald,' she said in a low voice, her hand again falling softly on his arm, 'I think you are fond of me; you have shown that you are, indeed, more than once.'

' No, I have not!' he burst out; 'I have no chance or opportunity of doing so! I only want to prove to you how much I love you! I hate the life you are leading, and I want to take you away from it—I hate to see you stared at by a lot of senseless gabies, who think they are patronising you by clapping their hands and thumping their infernal umbrellas. I hate to see these brutes of officers— we shall have them all here on Thursday night, I suppose—haw-hawing about the passages, and talking of you in their idiotic manner. I want to take you out of all this, I want to marry you and make you mine, and mine alone!'

'To marry me!' she said with a very sad smile. 'You forget, Gerald, that I am six years older than you, and that I shall be an old woman—'

'I knew you would say that! I hate it! You shouldn't say that,' he broke out impetuously. 'How many hundreds of men are there who have married women older than themselves, and lived perfectly happy lives! You make yourself older than you are by the hard work you do. I want to work for you, to slave for you, to make money that you may share it, to make a name that you may be proud of me; and I will do it yet. I am not always going to remain a drudge in a country theatre. I shall get the chance some day; and then, O, Madge, how proud I shall be of you as my wife!'

'You are a foolish boy,' she said, bending her deep hazel eyes full upon him, 'and must not talk to me in this way.'

'No,' he said, curling his lip and shrugging his shoulders; 'such talk is idle now, I know; I know I have nothing to offer now. If I ever had the chance of attaining a position, I would ask you to marry me; for then the knowledge that I was fighting for you would nerve me in the struggle ; and you would not say No to me then, would you, Madge?'

'You shall ask me when the chance arrives, Gerald,' said the girl in a low tone, 'and I will answer you then.'

'That time may be nearer than you imagine,' said the young man. 'Now, you have had a long day, and will have to begin again shortly. Let me see you to your home.'

It was Miss Pierrepoint's custom to lie down on her bed for an hour every afternoon before proceeding to the theatre, and thus prepare herself for the exertions of the evening. Visitors were refused admittance; perfect quiet reigned throughout the house; and Rose Pierrepoint sat in the drawing-room with the door open, ready to rush out and

scare away any chance irruption of cackling
poultry, barking dogs, or grinding organ-men.
On this day, however, though the house was
as quiet and Rose as vigilant as ever, Madge
Pierrepoint could not sleep. She lay outside
the bed, her long brown hair unloosed, hastily
combed off her face and floating over her
shoulders, her head resting on her hand, and
an odd wild gleam in her brown eyes.

'How wonderful,' she said to herself, 'how
wonderful that Gerald should choose to-day,
of all days in the year, to say what he just
said to me ! I knew that he was fond of me,
of course; I could not help knowing it; but
he had never spoken so plainly as he did just
now. What a contrast between what I heard
last night and what I heard to-day! Philip
grumbling at me for not making more money;
grumbling at the sum — little enough, but
hardly earned—which I am able to send to
him; dissatisfied because I have none of those
accomplishments which, as he seems to think,
alone go down with a London audience. And
then this boy, hating the mere fact of my be-

ing compelled to appear in public; writhing under the notion that my name is bandied about in men's mouths, and that I am a subject of discussion, however complimentary; anxious only to give me rest, and quite contented, as he says, to slave for me, and desirous only of fame that I may share it with him. And Philip tells me he "trusts me," and bids me dally with the boy's affection, and see how much money can be made out of him. To that baseness I will not stoop! I will put an end to this nonsense altogether; I will no longer listen to— And yet how wonderfully soft and tender his manner is! Heaven knows my life is hard enough—a grinding servitude, with only this one gleam of affection to light it up. And that I will not deny myself. No; the chance that Gerald talks of will never come. He will weary of me as Philip has wearied. Meanwhile, until he does weary of me, I will not deprive myself of his society— no, nor of his worship—the only sunshine in my life.'

CHAPTER IV.

FRIENDS IN COUNCIL.

THE income which Major Vane derived from his sporting transactions being of a fluctuating character, and the sum regularly transmitted to him by his wife being, as he justly considered, contemptible in amount, that gallant officer was unable to have his permanent home as luxurious, or even as comfortable, as he undeniably wished it to be. Though accustomed to speak of his abode vaguely and generally as his 'rooms,' the Major in reality occupied only one apartment, which was situate at the top of a house, the ground floor of which was a shop of such enormous dimensions, that it not merely absorbed the first and the second floors, but so bulged out at

the side as only to leave space for a private
door so narrow that it looked like one plank,
and for a staircase which was perfectly ladder-
like in the slimness of its proportions. In the
fanlight above the narrow door — so narrow
as to consist only of one pane of glass—and
immediately above the small speck of blue
gas that was allowed to issue from the one
tiny burner, was pasted in the off season a
fly-blown skimpy little bill, inscribed with a
legend, setting forth that apartments were to
be let 'for club gentlemen.'

In the off season only; for during the season the 'club gentlemen' mustered so strongly
as to render the announcement quite unneces-
sary. Of various kinds were they, and so
numerous, that one wondered where they
could find space sufficient to stow themselves
away. Blue-faced majors of the Bagstock
breed, with pendulous cheeks and double-
breasted coats and buckskin gloves, occasion-
ally took up their quarters in the 'apartments
for club gentlemen,' which also afforded shel-
ter to an Irish M.P., who was popularly sup-

posed to live upon the produce of the sale of
blue-books and printed parliamentary docu-
ments for waste paper, and whose tall hat
was so extremely shiny as to cause the parliamentary funny man—like most parliamentary funny men, but a poor joker—to say that
O'Dwyer must have forgotten to take his hat
off one morning when he greased his hair.
There, too, for three weeks, in the very height
of the season, sleeping for about two hours
out of the twenty-four, was to be found a provincial newspaper reporter, who spent all the
money and health which he had gained during the previous eleven months in rushing
about from theatre to concert, from dance to
drum, from artist's studio to author's library,
chatting, note-taking, observing, and gathering together an amount of anecdote and chit-
chat, upon the distinction due to the purveyor
of which he lived, a courted guest, on his return to his native town.

In the midst of this motley colony Major
Vane was the sole regular tenant. The bedroom which he inhabited, though at the top

of the house, was larger, airier, and better furnished than the rest, and he kept it on throughout the year; because, though he was often absent for weeks together, going from race-meeting to race-meeting, or staying in the country-houses of trainers and jockeys, with certain of whom he was a great favourite, he was always liable to be summoned to London, where he made it a point of having a *pied-à-terre.* There was a certain recklessness of tone about the whole affair which amused him. He laughed at the open note, written in a round hand by the landlady, and skewered on to the extinguisher of the Irish member's candlestick, informing that distinguished politician that the cabman who brought him from the House on the previous wet night had called twice, and would take out a summons unless the money was left for him in the morning. He grinned as he inspected the highly-scented notes, addressed in violet ink and very scrawly writing, which awaited the return of the blue-faced major. He laughed as he stumbled over the enormous high-lows

of the provincial newspaper reporter. He did
not mind the smell of warm mutton fat, tempered by tobacco, which lingered on the staircase. He did not mind the normal state of
blackness in which lived the female slave of
the establishment, who printed off impressions of her fingers and thumbs on everything which she could possibly clutch hold
of. He would have objected to her very
strongly, indeed, and to the black-beetles, in
whose company she lived, and which, when
dead, were in the habit of dropping out of
her costume as she moved along; and to her
cooking—an art which, judging from the result, she seemed generally to practise con-
temporaneously with the performance of her
toilet and the arrangement of her hair. He
would have objected to all this, had he had
anything to do with it. But the fact was,
that Major Vane only slept at his lodgings,
and ate, drank, wrote, read, played cards, received visits, and gave his address at his club.

·The Craven, to which Major Vane belonged, may best be described as a shady

club. It was situated on the shady side of the way, in a shady street, in the neighbourhood of Piccadilly, and the members were all more or less shady, generally more. There were shady majors, and colonels, and captains, some of whom had been in the regular service, which they had quitted in a remarkably shady manner, but most of whom were accredited by or attached to Indian nawabs, or foreign potentates of the shadowiest as well as the shadiest order. There were shady barristers, whose names were recollected in connection with the shadiest cases, and shady attorneys who employed them. Such members of the Craven Club as had well-known names, were for the most part the worst of all. Whenever one of those names was mentioned, the question arose, 'What have I heard about that man?' and the reflection was generally certain to bring something forward to the discredit of the gentleman in question.

One noticeable feature of the Craven Club, too, was that though most of its members were seen a great deal in public, driving

handsome horses in the park, lounging out
of pit-boxes at the opera, and sprawling in
stalls at theatres, always expensively dressed
in exaggeration of the reigning fashion—no
one ever met them in general society. They
gave each other elaborate banquets at the
club, they were seen during the season at
Richmond and Greenwich, entertaining ladies,
quietly dressed, and not indecorous in manner, who were equally unknown to the rest
of the London world. Sometimes they would
make an attempt to assert themselves. The
men would get themselves proposed for some
established and well-known club, when they
would be either black-balled or withdrawn.
The women would call upon some ladies
whose husbands had been introduced to them;
the visit would not be returned, and any further attempt at intercourse with the outer
world would for a time be abandoned.

Not that they would be discouraged at
these rebuffs. They ignored them as far as
possible, and when compelled to accept them,
they would shrug their shoulders, and talk

of themselves as Bohemians; though between their debased and sensuous lives and the honest, free Bohemianism of literature and art, there was as much resemblance as between their purple whiskers and painted faces and the black locks and bronzed cheeks of the real Romany.

In its external life, at least, the Craven had some resemblance to other clubs ; men ate and drank there, and there was a writing-room (the blotting-cases of which, if they could have revealed the secrets confided to them, would have been invaluable to Messrs. Moss and Moss, the attorneys of Thavies-inn, or Serjeant Skinner, the well-known leader in the Divorce Court), and a smoking-room, where many curious little 'plants' had been concocted, and a card-room and a billiard-room. The wines and spirits supplied to the members were undeniably good; Dick Wrangham, commonly known as Ringlet Wrangham, took care of that, for after he had sold out of the cavalry and failed as a horse-dealer, some of his friends set him up as the pro-

prietor of the Craven, and out of its profits
he earned a very tolerable income.

About noon on the second day after his
return from Wexeter, Major Vane entered
the club, and ordered his breakfast. In the
coffee-room he found several other members
engaged in discussing the same meal; breakfast, however, at the Craven Club, was by
no means of the ordinary kind. On the tables
was seldom to be seen any tea or coffee, or
their usual accompaniments; there was toast,
certainly, but it was prepared with anchovy;
there were devilled biscuits and cayenned
legs of poultry, and artful thirst - provoking
preparations of dried fish; and for the allay-
ing of the thirst when provoked, there were
cool cups, which on the whole were found
to inebriate considerably more than they
cheered, and effervescing liquors of all kinds.

Noon was the very earliest period of the
day recognised at the Craven Club; the number of members did not admit of more than
one staff of servants being kept, and as the
habits of its frequenters were undoubtedly

late, much alacrity before noon could not be
expected of the waiters who had not retired
to rest before daybreak. Very filmy - eyed
and cloudy-linened were these domestics in
the morning, as they yawned in the bay-win-
dows and swept up the fragments of cigar-
ash with dirty dusters, and plunged their
fingers into flat remains of half-emptied tum-
blers.   The grim old porter, who had an
easier time than most of them, as he slept
soundly during the latter part of the night
in his glazed box, always had a hoar frost
of silver beard upon his mottled cheeks, and
cursed, and envied while he cursed, the bright
freshness of the boy who slapped the newspapers down on the desk before him and
laughed in his face.   The man who brought
the play-bills knew something about sitting
up late, and the woman who left the milk
knew something about getting up early; but
in regard to the number of hours' sleep they
had, one might be regarded as Rip Van
Winkle, and the other as the Sleeping Beauty,
in comparison to this hall-porter.   By noon,

however, all the establishment was on the
alert ; the members who lived in lodgings
wanted their breakfasts, and the members
who lived at home, and who for various reasons did not care to have their correspond-
ence addressed to their private houses, wanted
their letters. There was generally great
anxiety to see the sporting papers, several
copies of which were taken in at the Craven,
and there were hazy reminiscences of last
night's conversation to adjust, and half-made,
half-dreamt-of wagers to regulate and settle.

All the men at breakfast looked up as
Philip Vane swaggered to the waiter's desk
to give his orders, and two or three of them
growled out 'Good-morning.' He was a popular man in the club, and had it been dinner
time, would have been received with a chorus
of acclamation, but the members of the Craven
were generally short - tempered and reticent
in the morning, and thought a nod quite sufficient greeting. Major Vane returned the
salutations in his usual careless, insolent way,
seated himself at his table, and buried him-

self in the folds of a sporting newspaper. From the vaticinations of the writer, whose principal merit appeared to be the ingenious manner in which he refrained from mentioning the name of the horse whose merits he was discussing, alluding to it now as the son of its sire, now as the native of the place where it was bred, and now as the property of the person who owned it, Major Vane's attention was distracted by the simultaneous arrival of his breakfast and of a friend.

There were some points of similarity and dissimilarity between them; the breakfast was sound and good, the friend was neither; the breakfast had to be paid for, so generally had the friend. There was a doubt as to whether the breakfast might disagree with one, there was no doubt about the friend's disagreeing with one, if by so doing he saw a chance of bettering his position. Delabole was the friend's name, his status that of gentleman, though twenty years before, when he spent a few happy days with Lieutenant Bird, the governor of Alnwick gaol, his name was Mun-

ker, his profession horse coping. But Alnwick was a long way off, and Lieutenant Bird
had been dead for many years.

A short fat man, Mr. Delabole, with a
square head like a tin loaf, no neck to speak
of, an enormous chest, always set off by a
very open shirt-front, or covered by a water-
fall of satin, with one valuable pin in its
centre; short awkward legs, and very small
hands and feet. The latter, which were flat
as well as small, always looked like the feet
of the dummies in the tailors' shops; the little
fingers of the former were always covered
to the knuckles with lustrous rings. Philip
Vane saw the rings blazing on his shoulder
before he looked round at their owner. Mr.
Delabole always put his hands on his friends'
shoulders and generally called them 'dear
boy.' He was a large-hearted man, very.

'We wanted you with us last night, dear
boy,' were Mr. Delabole's first words after
the interchange of greetings.

'And I wanted you here,' said Philip
Vane.

There was something in his look which aroused Delabole's attention, for he said quickly:

'Why, has anything been done?'

'Not much. Bolckoff brought his cousin here, the man from Germany, about whom he is always swaggering.'

'I know.'

'Well, I played écarté with him.'

'Well!'

'We played five games, of which he won three.'

'Ah! that means nothing, dear boy!' said Mr. Delabole, drawing up his chair, and dropping his voice. 'You were playing—'

'Foxey!' said Vane in a whisper; 'so was he, foxey to the teeth and eyes, foxey all over! Vine grower at Neuwied, Bolckoff called him, and thought I believed it! No Rhenish grape merchant ever handled his cards like that Viennese, my dear Delabole! As keen a Viennese sharp as ever swaggered in the Prater, or played at the Verein.'

Philip Vane's eyes flashed, and his voice

grew a little louder as he finished this sentence. Mr. Delabole held up a warning finger, and when he spoke there was no trace of emotion in his tone.

'It is very, very likely, dear boy!' he said, in a fat whisper; 'it's just one of Bolekoff's moves! Your Polish Jew, sir,' continued Mr. Delabole, shaking his head sententiously, 'your Polish Jew is a bad breed!' Then, in quite a different tone, he added, 'What did you want me for, dear boy?'

'Merely to know whether I was right as to our friend's style; merely to see whether you agreed with my idea of it.'

'No occasion for my presence for that; trust my Philip for the spot-stroke in such a case! For finding needles very judiciously hidden in bottles of hay, there is not, I believe, your equal.'

'You must want something of me very badly indeed, Delabole,' said Vane grimly. 'I never heard you so complimentary. Has it anything to do with last night, of which you were speaking?'

' It had nothing to do with anything in the world, dear boy,' said Delabole, ' certainly not with anything of last night, which was devoted to pleasure, and in which no trace of business intruded.'

' Pleasure !' repeated Philip Vane.

' Pleasure, and nothing else,' said Delabole. ' A delightful little supper given to Lotty Lopez, and a few of her female friends.'

' Ah !' said Philip Vane shortly.

' And why " ah !" dear boy ?'

' I don't go in for that sort of thing.'

' Perhaps not,' said Mr. Delabole, in his airiest manner; ' but because you are virtuous, are there to be no more cakes and ale? It was really a very pleasant little gathering, not the less so from the touch of romance attending the circumstances.'

' Romance ?' echoed Philip Vane, with a laugh. ' What was there romantic about it? Was the landlord so fascinated by Miss Lotty's beaux yeux, that he declined to take any money for the bill, or was the brilliancy so contagious that one of the waiters exhibited a talent which he had hitherto hidden under a napkin?'

'Neither, dear boy,' said Mr. Delabole quietly; 'nor was any one rude—as you are just now! Rudeness isn't clever, dear boy, and as a general rule doesn't pay. No; the little spice of romance was derivable from the fact that it was a farewell banquet to Lotty, who, with her little troupe, has been engaged by Wuff on a travelling tour for three years, and quits these shores for America next week.'

'What a blow for England!' said Philip Vane; 'how she will sigh over her departing. children!'

'There are others of her children,' said Mr. Delabole, 'who may some day be called upon to depart from her shores, under different circumstances, and whom she will not regard so much! As for myself, little Lotty always amused me, and I am sorry she is going; I could have better spared a better woman. That's a quotation, I believe, but, oddly enough, it's true.'

'If you are so fond of her, why don't you go with her?' said Vane.

'Because it wouldn't suit me, dear boy; because there is no opening for me; because —I don't want to, in point of fact. But, for the matter of that, why don't you? Wuff's at his wits' end for a leading man and leading woman. Let me write him a line, and say I have found the first in you?'

A sudden thought struck Philip Vane.

'Hold on a minute and drop chaffing. Does he really want a leading actress to go out with this lot with him? Not a dancing, capering wench, I mean, but a woman who can act?'

'He does want one most infernally.'

'What will he give?'

'Well, our friend Wuff isn't in the open-handed, melting, charity line, but I should think he would stand six pounds a week, and travelling expenses. He gives Lotty ten, I know, but then—'

'I'll find him the person he wants,' said Philip Vane quickly.

'You, dear boy?' said Delabole, surprised. 'I thought you said just now you were not in that line?'

'Nor am I, but when I was down in the West the other day, I saw a girl—Miss Pierrepoint, I think she was called—'

'Pierrepoint!' said Delabole. 'Yes, I've heard of her in the provinces. Good, isn't she?'

'So far as I understand these matters, very good,' said Vane; 'a friend of mine is interested in her.'

'Ah, ah,' said Delabole, 'we know what that means.'

Vane knew, too, what Delabole's tone meant; knew that it was his wife thus alluded to, but took no notice.

'I mean,' he continued, 'he should be glad to see her position improved, and this is an opportunity which I think would suit her.'

'I would, if I were you, dear boy,' said Delabole, looking at him straight in the face, 'I would just put on my friend's hat and my friend's coat, put my friend into the train, and get him to discuss the matter with Miss Pierrepoint.'

'You think that's devilish funny,' said Major Vane, returning his stare, 'but you're wrong for once. The woman is nothing to me, only I thought it might suit her, and do your friend a good turn at the same time.'

'All right, dear boy,' said Mr. Delabole. 'I will let Wuff know. If it comes off, she must start next week.'

'I have heard,' said Mr. Delabole to himself, as he climbed into the mail-phaeton which was waiting for him at the door, 'I have heard Philip tell a great many lies cleverly, but never so cleverly as that one he told just now. His face was a perfect study of candour. Pierrepoint? I'll make a little memorandum of this conversation when I get into the city.'

When Philip Vane had finished his breakfast, he went into the writing-room, and wrote this letter to his wife:

'*Thursday.*

'You need not send up the benefit money

to-morrow, I will come down and fetch it.
Meet me in the same place at the same time
to-morrow; I have something very important
to say to you.'

CHAPTER V.

Miss Pierrepoint's benefit was even a greater success than her warmest and most sanguine friends had anticipated. The dramatic critic of the *Wexeter Flying Post* remarked the next day that 'such a galaxy of beauty and fashion had never before been gathered together in our little temple of Thespis.'

And he was almost justified in his statement. The clerical party was fully represented. The bishop was away in London; but the dean was there, rosy and bland, following the text of the tragedy in a large quarto volume, which he had brought with him, beating time to the delivery of Mercutio's speech about Queen Mab as though he had been conducting an oratorio, and benignly deaf to the profane remarks with

which the representative of Colonel Hardy in
Paul Pry thought fit to season the author's
dialogue. Emboldened by their august leader's
presence and evident delight, the other pillars
of the church gradually relaxed from the ex-
treme state of severity into which they had
thought fit to settle themselves on their en-
trance, while the female members of their
families sighed over Juliet's woes, and tit-
tered at Phœbe's impudence, in unrestrained
freedom. Be sure that Probus, the coach-
maker and Shakespearian enthusiast, was in
the front-row with his family, looking as if
he knew all about the tragedy, and wagging
his head as one who should say, 'I am pleased
to see the delight it affords you, my friends,
but I have been steeped in it for many years.'
Gerald Hardinge was right in his anticipation
of the presence of the military. The officers
were there in force, from the colonel to the
youngest subaltern, and being one and all in
severe evening dress, gave quite an aristocratic appearance to that portion of the dress-
circle which they filled. So Sam Cave said,

at least, and Sam Cave ought to have known, having twice attended the performances of Madame Malibran in London, and being the only person within many miles who was supposed to know what Fop's Alley was, or what it meant.

The good townspeople, too, most of whom had heard from Miss Cave of her lodger's quiet life, and of the way in she supported her younger sister, made a point of attending in crowds, and of cheering the heroine of the evening to the echo. These cheers she really deserved, as, always conscientious and painstaking, she had never so thoroughly identified herself with any character, never so sunk her own individuality in the part to be assumed, as on this occasion. The extra excitement and fatigue, indeed, had so far prostrated her, that at the conclusion of the performance, Miss Cave, who had been checking the accounts in the front of the house, ran round to the stage-door, and seeing Gerald Hardinge in waiting on Miss Pierrepoint, bade him take her home at once, leave her at the door, and

not attempt to talk to her that night, and the
worthy soul added to Madge, ' You will not
see me, my dear, until to-morrow morning, or
hear anything from me about it; though I
can tell you that owing to Sam's having
packed them together like herrings, we have
got more money than I can ever recollect
into the house, and the result will be better
than I told you; I will come up to your room
the first thing to-morrow morning with the
amount.   And now, Mr. Hardinge, take her
off directly.'

The next morning, when Miss Pierrepoint
awoke, she found that the kind old lady had
already been to her room, for lying on her
pillow was a small white-paper parcel containing the items of the account jotted down
in Miss Cave's neat, though now tremulous
handwriting, and more than forty-eight pounds
in notes, gold, and silver.

Forty-eight pounds ! Madge counted it
over two or three times and was delighted,
for that was considerably more than she had
led Philip to expect.   How pleased he will

be! Perhaps he will be able to spare her a little of it; she would like to make old Miss Cave a present, and some acknowledgment to two or three others, who had put themselves to extra trouble and inconvenience on her account, and who could little spare the time they had given up. Rose, too, wanted a new gown sadly; Madge knew the girl was ashamed of her dress, though she never complained. But she had refused to go out walking very often lately, except in the evening dusk, and Madge was sure that was the reason. As Madge was in the midst of this wonderment, there came a knock at the door, and Miss Cave entered the room.

'That's a good girl,' said the old lady, looking not without admiration at the pretty figure before her, with its long brown hair floating over its shoulders; 'I thought you would not be foolish enough to get up just yet after all your fatigue, so I have brought you a letter which has just been left by the postman. There it is,' she continued, laying it on the bed, 'a letter with the London postmark and a smart seal; I only hope it is not from any London manager, who has heard of you and wants to offer you an engagement. Perhaps it's from Mr. Boscawen. I sent him one of your circulars, but I heard afterwards he had gone to London.'

'No,' said Madge, 'it isn't from a manager, and it isn't from Mr. Boscawen. It is not a very important communication. How very good of you, dear Miss Cave, to take so much trouble about me, and to get me all this money!' She looked up and tried to smile, but the light had died out of her eyes, and her lips trembled.

'No thanks at all, my dear,' said the old lady; 'it was your own talent and niceness that drew the money, and all I had to do was to collect it, and make it up for you. Now, if you don't want to sleep any more, I will make you a nice cup of tea, and bring it up to you before you dress.'

So soon as she was left alone, Madge took up the letter and read it again.

'What can it mean?' she said to herself.

'Philip knows I would send him the money at once and safely. I have done so before; it cannot be for that, then, that he is coming! There must be something important that brings him here so soon again! It's over-fatigue only, I suppose, but I am horribly low and down this morning, and feel as if something evil were going to happen.'

All day long the same wonder beset her. What could it be? And the apparent importance of it grew as she thought it over.

One thing was certain, she must meet him that night. There would be a difficulty, but that must be overcome. Gerald Hardinge would want to see her of course. Now and then, once a week, perhaps, he was in the habit of coming in when he had seen her home from the theatre, and partaking of their frugal supper with her sister and herself, a small but pleasant meal, to which, on such occasions, he always insisted on contributing.

He would want to come that night doubt-less. There were numerous incidents of the benefit to be talked over; she had scarcely

seen him since, and he would doubtless propose himself as a visitor that night. It could
not be. She must go and meet Philip, that
was imperative; she must devise some story
which would satisfy Gerald, and in order to do
that, Rose must be taken into her confidence.

That last necessity was very unpleasant
to Madge Pierrepoint. In the course of her
career, straight as she endeavoured to keep
it, she had to undergo various little shifts and
privations, to pass through various phases of
life, not necessarily base or ignoble in themselves, but rendered so by their connections
and surroundings. But all these were with
scrupulous care hidden from the knowledge
of her younger sister. Madge Pierrepoint
was not unacquainted with the mysteries of
the pawnbroker's shop; she had had experience of the hard bargains driven by the tally-
man for clothes which were absolutely necessary to her in her profession, and of the ex-
tortions of the usurer—not unfrequently some
other member of the company—for salary lent
to her in advance.

But Rose knew nothing of all these things. She was but a child, Madge said, and it was desirable that she should be kept as long as possible in ignorance of all the bad ways of this weary work-a-day world. She had her French lessons to do, with her music, and then there was her painting, in which she took such interest, and in which Gerald Hardinge so kindly helped her. Let her go on with this until the time came when she must struggle for herself; but until that time came, let the meanness and the shifts of hard-grinding poverty be kept from her.

Now, however, she must be taken into confidence, so far at least as to throw dust in the eyes of Gerald Hardinge and Miss Cave, both of whom would be curious as to Madge's proceedings. Madge recognised this, and thought out her plan of action while she dressed herself, and when she crossed over into her little sitting-room, she was perfectly prepared with it.

Rose was delighted to see Madge, and ran up and kissed her, and congratulated her on

the success of the benefit. Rose had never
seen Madge look so gloriously, or play so
splendidly, as she had done on the previous
night; and Miss Cave had told her that
Madge had made a lot of money; and that
was good hearing; for they wanted it badly
enough, goodness knows. 'Just look at my
rags,' said Rose in parenthesis, holding up her
arm, and showing where the poor cheap stuff
had undeniably frayed away. And Madge
must be awfully tired, mustn't she—good thing
she only played in the first piece that evening
—and she must come home directly after and
go to bed, and the next day there was no
rehearsal, and she could take a long rest, and
they could talk over all that was to be done.

There was Madge's chance. She replied
affectionately and sweetly to all her sister's
congratulations, and then she added, 'I was
very tired, dear, but I have had a good long
sleep, and I cannot come home early to-night,
as you suggest, because I have to go out for
an hour or two on a matter of business.'

Rose's face flushed instantly. 'Going out,

Madge, what again? You were out—when was it?—Monday night, the night of the storm. How very strange!'

'And I shall be out again and again, or I shall remain at home here without moving out at all, just whenever it suits my purpose, however strange you may think it, my dear Rose,' said Madge quietly.

'Well, but—'

'Be good enough to attend to me; I have business which calls me out to-night. It is probable that when Gerald Hardinge does not find me in the theatre, he will come on here.'

'O, then your business does not concern Gerald Hardinge?'

'My business concerns myself—and you— and no one else.' And Madge's cheek burned as she uttered the lie.

'O, I only thought — What then?' said Rose inconsequently, but much less acrimoniously than before.

'Well, if Gerald comes on here, you must tell him that I have gone to bed thoroughly tired out, but I will see him in the morning.'

'O, Madge! but suppose he sees Miss Cave?'

'If Miss Cave comes home before Gerald arrives, you must tell her the same story; if she comes after him, you will tell her that I have gone to Mrs. Probus's, who wanted especially to see me, and that I shall not be late.'

'But, Madge, won't it—'

'Do as I tell you, Rose, and don't ask any questions! Depend upon it that what I am going to do is both for your interest and mine.'

And Rose, who took a very different view of the affair when she found that Mr. Gerald Hardinge was not mixed up with her sister's proceedings, promised compliance, and said no more.

It was dull work that night at the theatre; *Romeo and Juliet* was played again, 'in consequence of its enormous attraction;' but no one who had been present on the previous night would have recognised the performance. Reaction was evident everywhere, even down

to the two 'supers,' and Mrs. Gonnop, who
played the Nurse. The house was not one-
third full, and those persons who were present seemed bored and dissatisfied. The curtain was no sooner down than Madge Pierrepoint ran to her dressing-room, threw a large
cloak over her stage-dress, dashed some water
over her face, twisted up her hair, put on her
bonnet, and sallied forth. She saw nothing
of either Miss Cave or Gerald Hardinge, but
turned rapidly into the street, and along the
road up which we have before tracked her
footsteps.

A very different night from that on which
she last went this expedition. Now all was
bright and clear, the moon riding high in the
blue sky, and every object in the landscape
standing out square and closely defined against
her light. Mellowed and softened by her rays,
the Dumpington-turnpike threw a shadow,
strange, foreign, and kiosk-like, over the road
into the little lane, the moonbeams penetrated
through interlacing trees, working a wavy
arabesque pattern on the green hedgerows,

and chequering the winding path with light and shade.

This time Madge was not the first to arrive. As she turned into the lane, a figure arose from the bank, against which it had been lying, and advanced to meet her. It was her husband.

'You're late,' was his genial greeting.

'I came away as soon as I could, Philip,' she replied; 'didn't even stop to change my dress—look here.' And she opened her cloak, showing Juliet's white robe underneath.

'By Jove,' he said, glancing at her, 'there's purity! What is it, a Druidical priestess, or a virgin of the sun?'

She flushed angrily for a moment, but recovered herself directly, then said with a short laugh, 'You would rather it were Iago's doublet, I suppose, and that I could not merely give you his counsel, "put money in thy purse," but act upon the advice. However, I can do that as it happens without the doublet. This is for you,' and she placed a small packet in his hand.

'What is this?' he exclaimed, as he took it. 'O yes, the benefit, I forgot all about it! How much is there here?'

'Forty-eight pounds, Philip,' she cried, laying her hand upon his shoulder, and looking up into his face. 'Isn't it good?'

'Might have been worse,' he said, quietly slipping the money into his pocket. 'Well, and how did it go off, and all that sort of thing?'

'I scarcely know what you mean by all that sort of thing,' said Madge; 'the house was very full, as you will know by the contents of your waistcoat-pocket.'

'Yes, but you? Did you tip 'em the word in grand style? Did you let 'em have it from the shoulder?'

'I spoke the text of the part, so that I conclude that I did tip them the word. I don't understand your delicate allusion to the shoulder.'

'There, don't be cross, Madge,' said Philip Vane, putting his arm round her; 'I know I am always talking slang, but that's the fault of the people I live with; I've no doubt you acted splendidly and got plenty of applause.'

'Old Mr. Probus wrote me a note this morning, declaring he had never seen Juliet better played, and he recollects Miss O'Neil.'

'Dear old Probus,' said Philip Vane. 'What will he take to drink? Seriously though, I am delighted to hear it. Well, and what have you got to say to me?'

'I thought it was to say something to me that you came down here,' said Madge; 'for my part I have not got much to say. O yes, Philip, one thing I want you to do, if you can, to spare me a little of that money.'

'O,' said Major Vane, 'a little of that money, eh?'

'A very little will do, Philip: there are two or three things that I absolutely must have in my theatrical wardrobe, and poor Rose has scarcely a gown to her back.'

'It seems to me a devilish hard thing that we should have to provide poor Rose's gowns out of our income,' said the Major; 'however, of course, she can't be allowed to disgrace the family. Let me see,' he added, taking the packet from his pocket. ' What did you say the figure was?'

' Forty-eight pounds,' said Madge.

' Forty-eight. Five, ten, fifteen, ah, very neatly made up, forty-five in notes and three in gold. Well, Madge, I will see if I can spare you the three pounds, though I must confess that just now it is deuced inconvenient.'

Madge took the three sovereigns without a word. The devils of passion and wounded pride were struggling within her, and she dare not trust herself to open her lips.

' And, by the way,' continued Philip Vane, ' it was upon the very subject of money that I have come down to talk to you. You know all this applause and all these compliments from old Potbus, or whatever his name is, are very well in their way, but there is nothing substantial about them. The only way to appreciate a thing is by its money value, and the salary you are earning just now is an uncommonly small one.'

'When you say "appreciate a thing," you mean appreciate me by my money value, I suppose,' said Madge, 'and that to you is small. You must permit me to say, however, that you knew what it was when you condescended to accept it; and that it has not deteriorated since.'

'Yes,' said Philip Vane impatiently, 'all right! Just come off the high ropes, will you, and let's talk this thing through quietly, and in a business-like way. Our interests are the same, or ought to be.'

'Yes,' said Madge bitterly, '"or ought to be"!'

'Now, if I were not the best-tempered man in the world, you really would put me out by your interruption! Our interests are the same, and what is good for you is good for me. Now I have an idea, which, if I can only carry it out, will improve both your position and our interests.'

'Not by my going to London, Philip; not by my attempting to play in burlesque, and sing songs. O, for goodness' sake, don't ask me to do it! It would not be of the smallest use either; I should make a dead flat failure of it, and lose the little fame I have gained in my present humble way.'

'My good girl, I am not going to do anything of the sort. I would not dream of inflicting upon you such a degradation! On the contrary, what I have to propose entirely arises from the fact that you are what you are, a leading actress, and not one of those jigging jades.'

'Do you mean to say you have heard of an opening for me in my own line in London, Philip?' cried Madge eagerly.

'Well, no, not in London exactly,' said Major Vane

'Liverpool or Manchester?' she asked.

'No, wrong again; a little farther off. The fact is, that Mr. Wuff, whose name I daresay you have heard, a man who has been mixed up in theatrical matters for the last hundred years, I believe, has been organising a troupe to go out under his supervision to America, Australia, and other places of that kind, on a

three years' tour. He has made his arrangements with the best ballet people and that
sort of thing, and he wants some one for a
star actress, and I have come down to propose
that you should go.'

Madge had been listening open-eyed and
open-mouthed. When he ceased, she was si-
lent for a moment; then her first words were,
'But what of Rose?'

'O, damn it,' cried Major Vane, 'must she
go too?'

'She must, of course. How could I leave
her, with whom could I leave her? Of course
she must go!'

'Well,' said Major Vane, after a moment's
reflection, 'I daresay that could be managed.'
Wuff will make her play pages' parts, or turn
her into something useful, he thought to himself.

'Three years,' said Madge reflectively;
'it's a long time to be away. Do you think
you could manage to live without seeing London, and London acquaintances, and London
ways, for three years, Philip?'

'No,' said that gentleman candidly, 'I am certain I could not.'

'But you will have to, if we accept this offer?' said Madge.

'Eh?' cried Major Vane, in a loud and startled tone; 'you don't imagine that I am going away to play a leading lady too, do you?'

'Do you mean to say that you are not going, Philip?'

'I have not the remotest intention of doing anything of the sort; my business engagements here, my good girl, would prevent me.'

'O,' said Madge quietly, 'your proposition, then, relates to me alone?'

'Exactly!'

'You don't expect me to give you an answer here, and at once, I suppose?'

'Well, I did, as I rather want to get back to London.'

'It is impossible! It is a matter which will take serious reflection. If you are so pressed you had better go; I will write to you my decision.'

'No,' said Philip Vane promptly, 'that won't do; you must make up your mind, please, within the next twelve hours,' looking at his watch. 'It is now eleven o'clock; at eleven o'clock to-morrow morning I will be here again, and you will be good enough to meet me. Consider it thoroughly, and don't act upon impulse; your reply may have a greater influence on your future than you are at present aware of. Now, good-night.'

He did not offer to embrace her; he did not even approach her; but kissed the tips of his fingers airily, and walked off.

Madge, standing in exactly the same position, heard the rumble of the departing wheels of the cab which, as before, he had left at the bottom of the lane; then, with sad face and rebellious heart, she made the best of her way towards what she called her home.

CHAPTER VI.

When Madge Pierrepoint arrived at her lodgings, she found the door open, and Miss Cave looking down the street.

'At last, my dear,' said the old lady; 'I thought you were never coming; I have got the fidgets upon me to-night, and have been up two or three times to look out for you; and when I heard your footstep coming round the crescent—I would know it in a thousand —I thought I would wait, and get a little fresh air until you came up. Now in with you and get to bed at once; what with last night and all, you must be dog-tired.'

'And I am very tired, Miss Cave,' said Madge, with a faint smile.

'Tired, my dear; I have no patience with

that old Probus keeping you up to this hour. Was he pleased with what you did last night?'

' Very much pleased indeed,' said Madge, recollecting the letter she had received from the Shakespearian enthusiast; ' he said he had not seen anything like it since Miss O'Neil.'

' Did he ? Now, come, that was very civil of him, and not bad judgment either, for I saw her myself, and you resemble her in many points. Come now, my dear, you are dropping off to sleep, just you O'Neil off to bed.'

And the good old woman, closing the door, took Madge gently by the shoulder, and pushed her before her up the stairs.

On the dressing-table, in Madge's room, lay a twisted slip of paper. She took it up and read in Rose's handwriting :

' G. H. was greatly disappointed at not finding you to-night. He has something very particular to say to you; he will be away all day to-morrow. He says he will see you in the evening, and you must keep yourself dis-engaged, as it is most important. I wonder what it is: you will tell me, Madge, won't you?'

When Madge had finished reading the paper, she smoothed it out mechanically between her hands, laid it on the table again, and seated herself on the edge of her bed. The words which she had just perused made no impression on her mind. Her thoughts went back to the interview she had gone through, and as she recollected Philip Vane's last speech, her face grew gray, and set, and rigid, and her hands almost involuntarily locked themselves together in front of her.

' Not the remotest intention of going with me! that was what he said; his business engagements would prevent him. His business engagements! So that I am to go away to America, Australia, or to any other place where my employers may choose to take me, and he is to remain at home. I am to be thrown into such society as I may chance to meet, to make my own way as best I can, and he, the only person in the world to whom I can look, or ought to look, for advice, consolation,

or help, is to remain here, consoling himself
for my absence by the receipt of a larger
income derived from my earnings, which he
will undoubtedly take every means to secure.
It is too low, too mean, too unmanly!

'To go away by myself to the other end
of the world for three years, that is what he
asked me! I will not do it, come what may,
I will not do it! I have been too patient
and too quiet as it is; I have slaved for him
ungrudgingly, unrepiningly, in the knowledge
that I was his wife, and in the ridiculous
hope that his acknowledgment of my position was merely a matter of time. Now he
proposes to get rid of me for three years,
and with such a man as Philip Vane, it is
not difficult to understand what that means.
Three years! But only two have elapsed
since we were married, and even in that
short time my attraction for him has so
waned, my hold on him has so relaxed, that
he makes me such a proposition as this.

'What is it?' she cried suddenly, stepping
leisurely across the room, and looking at her-

self in the looking-glass on the dressing-table. 'Have I grown plain, old, or repulsive? I confess I cannot see the alteration,' she added proudly, shaking her hair back, after a moment's inspection of herself; 'nor if Mr. Philip Vane thinks so, is his opinion shared by every one. Here,' laying her hand on Rose's crumpled note, 'here is evidence to the contrary. Here is some one younger, better looking, and, unless I am very much mistaken, better bred, than Mr. Philip Vane, who would give all that he holds dearest in life for the companionship which that gentleman despises! Another example, God knows not wanted, of the misery set forth in those words, "too late." If I had only known Gerald Hardinge —I talk like a fool! Gerald Hardinge is a boy, who is nothing to me, and Philip Vane is—my husband.'

Her husband! The mere sound of the word sent her thoughts into a different current. Philip Vane was still the principal figure, not as she had just seen him—cold, sneering, practical, and hard — but ardent, romantic, and impassioned. Chepstow Castle and the path along the windings of the silver Wye, the young man so different in the polished ease of his demeanour, and the style of his conversation, even in the fit of his clothes, and his graceful negligent manner of carrying himself, from any one she had ever seen before. The stolen interviews, the long walks, finally the quiet marriage, with the local fisherman and his wife as the only witnesses; all these scenes and imaginations came floating across her brain and mysteriously served to still the storm which was raging within her breast. Philip could not mean what he had said; he could not think of parting with her for three years! It was to try her, perhaps, that he had suggested it; and she had fallen so readily into the trap. Perhaps she, too, was to blame; her place was by his side, and she ought to have tried to fall in with his proposition for her going to London. She would agree to that now, she would tell him so to-morrow, and then there would be no more questions of her going abroad, and the old happy time, the time of two years ago, would come back again. And so thinking, Madge Pierrepoint fell asleep.

These kindly feelings, these hopes for the future, had not passed away when Madge awoke in the morning. On first opening her eyes, indeed, the sense of some impending calamity, which she had felt so strongly on the receipt of Philip's last letter on the previous morning, haunted her again; but when she recollected her recent thoughts, and her determination to submit herself to her husband's wishes, so far at least as accepting an engagement in London was concerned, she speedily got the better of her weakness, and had not much difficulty in persuading herself that a happy future was yet in store for her. So, full of hopes and anticipations, she started forth soon after she had finished her breakfast. She knew that at that time she need fear no interruption from Rose, who during the whole of the morning was busy with her various lessons, or from Miss Cave, who, after the ordering of her little household, invariably set forth to take her place in the box-office of the theatre, a position which just then claimed her attention even more rigidly than usual, as the season was about to terminate, and all outstanding accounts had to be carefully gone through.

Madge knew, moreover, that at such an hour she should be able to walk through the streets without undergoing the severe scrutiny which was usually bestowed upon her. The good people of Wexeter, though better bred than those of many other provincial towns, were yet human. Consequently, the sight of anybody whom they recognised as connected with the theatrical profession, when attired in ordinary costume, and proceeding through the streets in an ordinary manner, awoke in them an amount of curiosity which betrayed itself, even amongst the highest and most refined, in covert glances, amongst the less delicate in prolonged stares, and amongst the boys in loud shouts of recognition and war-whoops of a wild character, indicative of a desire on the part of the shouters to make

an onslaught on the persons observed, and to
ascertain by pinches and other manual ap-
pliances whether they were really flesh and
blood. Miss Cave, indeed, had a legend which
she was accustomed to narrate on special occasions, setting forth that within the memory
of her father, the actors had been known as
'lakers,' and that on any of them being recognised in the streets, the cry of 'The lakers,
the lakers!' would call forth the utterance of
the ferocious hint to 'smash their heads agin
the wall.' This, however, was in the dark
ages; and now the recognised members of
the company were only subjected to a great
amount of staring and whispered observations,
generally of a complimentary character.

Even from this torture—for torture it was
to a sensitive-minded woman—Madge Pierrepoint was free during her early walk. It was
a tacitly-recognised tradition among the Wexeter people, that no one was to be seen in the
streets until the afternoon. The members of
the cathedral, their families, and a few ladies,
old and young, regularly attended morning

service, before and after which the female heads
of families might have been seen discharging
their marketing duties; but the generality of
these persons, constituting what was called society in the good old town, never appeared in
public until after that meal, which by a polite
fiction passed as luncheon, but which in most
cases was understood to be dinner.

Thus, when Madge reached the lane at the
back of the Dumpington turnpike, she found
the spot almost as much deserted as on the
previous night, scattered parties of working
people in the distant fields being the only human creatures within view.

Eleven o'clock rang out from the cathedral
as she arrived within sight of her destination;
and on hearing the sound, she quickened her
pace; and when she turned into the little lane,
her heart was beating fast, and her face was
all aglow. She was compensated for her hurry,
however, by finding that she was first at the
spot; and it was not until after she had taken
two or three leisurely turns up and down, re-
covering her breath, that she heard the sound

of wheels, and looking round, saw Philip Vane alight from a cab by the turnpike, and advance towards her.

That Major Vane was not in a very good temper, was evident from his first words.

'You are going to tell me that I am late, I suppose,' he said; 'but you need not, because I know it. Not that i overslept myself, or anything of that sort. How anybody sleeps at all in that infernal hotel, is a matter of wonder to me; it's a sin and a shame that a place like that shouldn't have something better than such a pothouse for a gentleman to put up at.'

'I wasn't going to say a word about your being late, Philip; I am only sorry to hear you were not comfortable at the Half Moon. Everybody speaks so well of the house.'

'It may be all very well for bagmen, and people of that kind,' said Major Vane, with great disgust.

'It has the reputation of being very clean,' said Madge.

'Clean!' echoed the Major; 'I knew you would say that. When people can say nothing

else for an inn, they say it's clean. Just as
when they can say nothing else for a man, they
say he is good-natured. All I know is, the
beds seem as if they were stuffed with potatoes
instead of feathers; and they give you cotton
sheets—cotton sheets, by Jove!'

'Well, it was only for one night, Philip,'
said Madge soothingly. 'To-day you will be
able to go back to your London luxuries.'

'My London luxuries—while you struggle on here! Is that what you mean to convey?' said Philip Vane, looking at her sharply.

'No, indeed, I did not mean to convey
anything of the kind,' said Madge quietly; 'I
meant no sneer. And, indeed,' she added, with
a desperate effort at cheerfulness, 'I do not
intend you to enjoy those luxuries, if luxuries
they be, much longer by yourself. I intend
to come up and share them with you.'

'The deuce you do!' said the Major in a
loud key. 'O, you have been thinking over
what I said to you last night, then?'

'I have.'

'What is the result of your deliberation?'

'I will tell you, Philip; but before I tell you, let me say one word about myself, about ourselves. I have been thinking a great deal, not merely about this one proposition, but about our lives altogether; and it strikes me that, for the last few months at all events, there has been a sort of division between us; not expressed, indeed, but nevertheless existing, which should not be. Our interests are one, and our great point in life should be to carry them out by working together loyally, and in unison. Do you follow me, Philip?'

He was standing with his face turned towards her now, but with his eyes looking far away over her shoulder, swaying himself to and fro, and switching his legs with a small cane which he carried in his hand.

'O yes, I follow you!' he said; 'it isn't time for me to speak just yet, while you are dealing in generalities. I am waiting until you come to the point, before I have my little say.'

Madge winced as he spoke, but took no farther notice. Then she proceeded:

'I have no doubt that I have been very
foolish in allowing my fears to get the better
of me, and in refusing to go and act in London. It must seem ridiculous to you that I
should be wasting what remains to me of my
youth and energy in playing to provincial au-
diences, and in earning so small a salary. I
can fully understand that, from what you saw
of me two years ago, you imagined that I
should by this time have made much greater
progress, and been enabled to contribute much
more effectively to our income. You shall
not have that cause for complaint any longer.
I will not even refuse to appear in any style
of character which your good sense and knowledge of the world may decide that I should
undertake with a chance of success; I will
give up any scruples of the kind which I have
hitherto held, and if you will get me an engagement — and I am sure, amongst all the
people you know, there must be plenty who
would be proud to oblige you — I will go to
London.'

She looked up into his face as she said

these last words, and made a slight movement
of her hand towards him, as though expect-
ant of some little recognition of her speech.
In this, however, she was disappointed. Major
Vane merely stopped himself in the act of
switching his legs, and looking down at her,
said,

'You seem to have mistaken what I said
to you last night; there was no question of
going to London in the matter.'

'No, not in what you last proposed, I
know; but you have said more than once that
you wished I would go to London, and now
I am not merely willing, but anxious to do so,
Philip.'

'It seems impossible to get you women to
be business-like,' said Major Vane pettishly.
'I took the trouble to come down here yesterday, bringing you an offer, which I should
have thought you would only have been too
glad to have availed yourself of, and given me
my reply at once. You demanded time for
deliberation, and I accorded it. Now, when
you should communicate to me your de-

cision, you branch off upon a totally different topic.'

His tone was harsh and morose; his manner half scornful, half savage. As Madge listened to and looked at him, all her recently-formed resolutions of submission, all her growing hopes for peace in the present, and happiness in the future, melted away. If such were to be the response to all her overtures of affection, they had been made for the last time.

Hurt, proud, and defiant, she threw her head back, and said with as much calmness as she could call to her aid,

'Since you wish our relations to be merely on a strict business footing, you will find me prepared to meet your wishes so far. You ask me if I will accept a three years' engagement to travel with a theatrical company through America and Australia, you during that time remaining in England. Do I state the matter rightly?'

'With almost legal precision,' said Major Vane with a sneer.

'Then to that proposition I answer, No,

no, no! See here, Philip Vane: I came to you this morning prepared to do my best to set matters right between us; to meet you more than half way; to give you, if it were possible, even more freedom than you have now; and not to attempt to claim my position until I had made such a name in London as would render you not ashamed to acknowledge me. To this separation—for such the Australian scheme really is, call it by what name you like—I could not have consented; but it might have been modified in some way, or if you had been kind and gentle with me, I—God knows—I might have gone away. But,' she added, speaking slowly, and curling her lip, and looking him full in the face, 'when you allow your hard bed and cotton sheets to influence your temper so far as to make you forget, not merely the regard due to me as your wife, but the respect which I should claim as a woman, I meet you on your own ground, and distinctly refuse to accept this offer which you have made me.'

'O, you do, do you?' said the Major slowly,

giving his legs one vicious switch; 'don't let's have any mistake about it this time; let me understand you quite clearly. You refuse?'

'I do!' she cried, exasperated at the mocking tone in which he spoke; 'I do, and I tell you so plainly. Do you think I have been blinded by this pretext for an instant? Do you think that I do not see plainly enough that your object is to rid yourself of me, apparently for a time only, but really for ever?'

'Well, and suppose it were?' he said quietly.

'Suppose it were!' she echoed; 'well, then, I tell you plainly. I would frustrate it. Do you hear? There is a devil I have in me, which, once roused, renders me a match for you, long-headed and crafty as you are.'

'Nice style of woman this, by George!' muttered Major Vane, low, but loud enough for her to hear.

'If she is not a nice style of woman, she has only you to thank for it,' cried Madge. 'What she is, you made her; for what she will be, the responsibility will rest on you. If you were a different style of man, I would speak to you in a different way. I would appeal to you, for God's sake, to remember what we are to each other, and to avert this ruin of soul and body which is overhanging us by acknowledging me, and giving me a portion, a very small portion, of your life. But to you I simply say that I am your wife; that I shall claim the position which the law will award me; and that any attempt of yours to disown or get rid of me will be fruitless and vain.'

As she uttered these last words, she emphasised them by stamping her foot and throwing out her hand. It was a natural movement with her; but scarcely had she made it before she grew hot and flushed, knowing to what taunt she had exposed herself. Philip Vane was much too brutal to neglect such an opportunity.

'*Brava, brava!*' he cried, clapping his hands softly together. 'Deuced good that! Always keep your energy for your peroration. You really have improved wonderfully;

and I am deuced sorry, for Wuff's sake, that
you decline to astonish—not the natives, but
the colonists. Now to business. You have
been remarkably candid with me; I will be
equally frank with you. In the first place,
the fact, which you make such a point of
asserting, and which you look upon as your
trump card—that I am your husband—would
be the very thing which would upset your
apple-cart and ruin your play. I have only
to prove that I *am* your husband, and the
law, which you were good enough just now
to threaten to evoke, will give me the power
of forcing you to accept this very excellent
offer, which you refuse so contemptuously.'

'I don't believe it.'

'Exactly. I thought you wouldn't; and,
unfortunately, it isn't a question which we
shall be able to bring to any issue, as I don't
intend to assert my conjugal rights. You
have happened to hit with remarkable dex-
terity the right nail on the head: I did intend
our little separation to be not merely temporary, but final. Oddly enough, I intend it still.'

'You may intend it,' said Madge bitterly; 'but you cannot carry it out.'

'There,' said the Major, giving his leg a few persuasive taps, 'there we differ. I rather think I can. You are my wife—understand, I admit that at once. If, to speak after the pleasant fashion which you have adopted —if you had been another style of woman, I might have been more reserved. I might have introduced a little innocent deception into the matter; have told you, as they do in novels, that our marriage isn't a legal one, either because the parson was a postman in disguise, or that I was a Quaker, while you were a Protestant, or some ingenious stratagem of that kind. But with you I do nothing of the sort; I fully admit the legality of our marriage; while at the same time I bid you a respectful farewell.'

'What do you mean?'

'Simply this : that by a method more speedy, more efficacious, and less expensive than any known to your friend the law, I dissolve this marriage between us. And I will be generous enough to let you into my plan, which is as simple as it is excellent. From this day forth you will never look upon me again. I disappear—efface myself, as the French say. Don't ask me how, because I scarcely know myself yet. I may emigrate; I may go abroad; may join Wuff's company as the Bounding Brother of something or other. I don't know what I shall do; but I do know this, that you will never see me again. Listen now, Madge Pierrepoint,' said he, suddenly changing his tone; 'for Madge Pierrepoint you are once again. I have been talking in a light tone; but I have meant every word I said—every syllable, by George! Our marriage is known to no one but ourselves; and when we decide upon ignoring it, it is just as though it had never happened. I will never interfere with your plans and projects. I swear that. But on your part you must leave me free. I need say nothing about that, however; for you will have no choice in the matter.'

He wheeled round, and walked rapidly

away without turning his head. Had he looked round, possibly he might have felt some touch of compunction or compassion; for he would have seen his wife lying sense-less on the ground.

CHAPTER VII.

GERALD'S LUCK.

THE Dumpington turnpike-keeper—a man
naturally of a pleasant and social disposition,
and inclined secretly to repine at the dulness
of the life to which circumstances had rele-
gated him—was in the habit of killing time
by gazing out of one or other of the square
panes of glass let in at either side of the toll-
house, and wondering what would be the next
object likely to present itself for the relief of
his monotony. The dust left by the passing
by of a flock of sheep yet lingered in the air;
and the turnpike-man had derived at least
five minutes' amusement in watching the manner in which the sheep had at first blindly
refused to go through the gate, dashing off
in every other direction, sticking their heads

into the hedgerows, bleating in a remonstrating manner, which was ineffective perhaps from being carried on in one note, notwithstanding the shake with which it concluded, and in seeing them finally, after having been run over by a very circus-rider of a dog, being hustled through the gate ignominiously on three legs, the fourth remaining in the hands of the driver or his assistant boy. The turnpike-keeper, with these reminiscences fresh in his mind, and a vacuous smile on his face, suddenly descried a new object of interest.

This was a woman advancing slowly, and with wavering footsteps. Her dress was covered with dust, and her hat was crushed and bent. When the turnpike-man first saw her, her veil was off, and her head thrown back as if to catch the air; but, as she approached, she pulled the veil over her face, and seemingly nerving herself for what she had to do, tried to steady her footsteps, and advanced with a swifter and surer pace. With more delicacy than could have been expected from

him, the Robinson Crusoe of the highway
gave up his first idea of addressing her, it
being his custom, for the mere sake of hearing the sweet music of speech, to accost every
passer-by, and did not even look after her
until she was through the gate, and some
distance on the road to the town. Then,
standing at his door, and scientifically, with
his little finger, plumbing the depths of his
pipe-bowl preparatory to filling it anew, the
worthy man muttered to himself:

'She had had a downer, she had; was all
covered with dust, and went very shaky on
her legs. Queer case that; respectable-look-
ing woman, too respectable for a tramp, but
been on the drink like the rest of 'em. That's
what ruins 'em all—the drink. If it hadn't
been for the drink, my wife would have been
here now, sitting in that easy-chair, and giving me a bit of her mind probably. Ah, well,
the drink ain't so black as he's painted; but
he had laid hold of that poor creature that
went by just now, surely.'

And the toll-keeper, turning back into the

house, proceeded to fill his pipe from the capacious stomach of a brown earthenware image which stood on his chimney-piece, with the full conviction that the woman he had just seen go by was drunk.

That woman was Madge Pierrepoint; and after a cursory glance at her, most people would have been of the toll-keeper's opinion. When she had passed beyond the ken of such as might be within the toll-house, she threw back her veil and raised her head well aloft again, once more dropping into the slow and wavering pace. It was with difficulty, indeed, that she managed to make any progress; for her knees trembled beneath her, and her vision was so dim and flurried as to necessitate her stopping after every few paces, and pressing her hands tightly before her eyes.

In these short intervals of rest the recollection of what she had just gone through would come back upon her: the vision of her husband confronting her, with a sneer upon his lips, would stand out terribly distinct; some of his words, the cruellest and most bitter of them, would surge up in her ears. Then, knowing that another instant's abandonment of herself to such thoughts would cause her again to faint away, with one strong act of will she would dismiss them from her mind, and doggedly plod on her way. Later on 'she would think of all this, go through it bit by bit, sift out what it meant, and determine what she ought to do; later on, when there was a bed near on which she could fall back and rest, a hand near to steady her or to smooth her forehead, a voice to tell her that she was not all alone in the world, and that though she had been deserted— No, no; that no one must ever know. But she was weak now, and could not think it out properly. Only let her get home.

So on through the quaint old streets, quiet and deserted now; for it is one o'clock, and at that hour Wexeter dines. The cathedral dignitaries are taking their luncheon in pleasantly shaded rooms, with low ceilings and black oak fittings, where generations of cathedral dignitaries had done precisely the same

thing at precisely the same hour. The ill-
used hard-worked notes of the long-legged
narrow-bodied pianos in the establishments
for young ladies at South-Hedge have ceased
to sound; for the young ladies are now engaged in attacking roast mutton with an appetite which they will speedily learn to be
ashamed of. And afterwards there will be
an hour's walk in the garden, with their arms
lovingly entwined round each other's waists,
and their mouths filled with little backbitings
and jealousies, before the overture to *Semi-
ramide* bursts forth upon the scent-laden air,
to the delight of the invalid old gentleman
who has taken lodgings in that quarter for
quiet and repose. Peacefully sleeps Mrs.
Twiddle, original manufacturer of the celebrated Bonneton lace; and three doors off,
equally peacefully, sleeps Miss Grylls, her late
assistant and present rival, behind the wire-
blind in her shop-window, on which the word
'from' is painted so very small, and 'Twiddle's'
so very large. Nothing is to be seen of the
proprietor of the photographic and religious

fancy - assortment shop, where you may pick
up a neat ecclesiastical book-marker for thirty
shillings, or a reduced copy in stone of the
ancient abbey font, handy to keep rings and
shirt-studs in, for five pounds. Slumber, too,
his young men, who wear white cravats and
black coats, and look like curates. Only one
verger, standing at the cathedral door—for
there is a train due about this time, and it is
a likely day for excursionists — sees Madge
Pierrepoint crossing the yard under the shade
of the great elm-trees, where the rooks are
holding a noisy concert over her head, and
he does not recognise her. Her progress has
been slow, but unwatched; and at length she
has reached her own door.

Madge longs for rest and quiet; but she
is not to enjoy them yet. At the foot of the
stairs she is confronted by Miss Cave. The
old lady has just returned from a long morning's work at the box - office, having gone
through all the accounts of the closing season,
having paid away and received to the utter-
most farthing, and having been able to submit

a very satisfactory balance-sheet to Mr. Dobson the manager. Naturally, therefore, she is in a good temper, and anxious to relieve herself, after the tedium of business, by a pleasant chat with her lodger, who is such a favourite with her.

'Why, where have you been, my dear?' said Miss Cave, holding up her hands as her eyes fell upon Madge's dust-covered dress. 'Not been knocked down by one of those dreadful cows, surely?' the idea of being tossed, gored, and trampled upon by errant cattle ranking foremost amongst the old lady's self-inflicted troubles.

'No, Miss Cave,' said Madge with a faint smile, looking down at her dress and endeavouring to brush the dust off with her hand; 'no, I have only been for a country walk, and, feeling a little tired, sat down in the hedgerow, without particularly observing where I placed myself.'

'Well, my dear, what you can want with taking long country walks, after all the work you have gone through, I cannot understand.

I can't say I think much of the country; for what with the cows and the dust and the crowds of midges that buzz all about you, it seems to me to be more pain than pleasure, taking it altogether. Now, when I go out of Wexeter, give me the seaside, I say; and, talking of that, my dear, I have brought some news which I think will please you.'

'Indeed, Miss Cave; and what might that be?'

'Well, Mr. Dobson is finely delighted at the success of his season—as well he may be, as being the best he has had the last three years. And when he said so to me just now, I up and told him at once that it was all owing to you, my dear, and that he had had no leading lady here for years that was a patch upon you, and that you were as great a favourite out of the theatre as in it.'

'That was very kind of you, dear Miss Cave.'

'It was only the truth, Madge—there, I never called you Madge before, not being given to use Christian names freely, as I find

is the custom in music-halls and low places
of that kind; but as I am fond of you, I will
do so now and in future—it was only the
truth, Madge; and Mr. Dobson agreed to it;
and then he asked me how I thought it would
do if he was to take the Avonmouth Theatre
for the short summer season; that would take
in the regatta and the races and the grand
military review. "Miss Pierrepoint would be
new at Avonmouth," he said; "and I think
she would draw." I told him I thought so
too; but that he must give you better terms
than you had here; for there would be the
expenses of moving for yourself and your
sister; and you would have perhaps to dress
a little more than you do here, it being a gay
place. Dobson didn't see it at first; but I
held to it. So finally he told me to talk to
you about it, and offer you an extra pound a
week.'

Miss Cave had expected that her announcement would be received with great pleasure.
She was disappointed when Madge, with a
grave face, said:

'I am much obliged to you, dear Miss
Cave, and to Mr. Dobson; but I don't think
the offer would suit.'

'Not suit you! You are too shy and
timid, Madge. You dislike going among
strange people; and perhaps you are afraid
of the officers and flighty fellows that you
have heard of in Avonmouth. Don't you be
afraid of them, my dear. Dobson wouldn't
dream of going without taking me with him;
and I shall be sure to look after you.'

'No, indeed, it isn't that.'

'Indeed, what can it be, then? O, I know
—that young Hardinge.'

'Mr. Hardinge? What about him?'

'Well, Dobson wanted him to go too.
The Avonmouth Theatre has not been open
for two years now, and the scenery all wants
looking after and touching up; and Dobson
wanted young Hardinge to go off in advance,
and get it ready by the time you came there;
but when he was spoken to this morning, he
said he was very sorry he could not, that his
engagement was up, and that he did not think

there was any chance of his coming back to the circuit.'

'And what has that to do with me, dear Miss Cave?'

'Well, my dear, I have got eyes in my head, though they are not so bright as they were, and I can see that while that young man is desperately in love with you, you have a sneaking kindness for him; and I thought you might have set your horses together, and—'

'Mr. Hardinge hasn't spoken to me on the subject, dear Miss Cave; and I assure you I have not the smallest knowledge of his movements.'

'Well, my dear, no offence. I won't take your answer to Dobson just now, lest you might change your mind. Think it over and let me know to-morrow; and if I were you, I would lie down a bit after dinner and rest myself. You ought to be very brilliant to-night; for it is not only the last night, but Dunsany's benefit; and he's sure to have a fine house; for he's a Buffalo, or a Druid, or something of that kind; and we shall be full of brothers, with aprons on, and green ribbons and tin thing-a-me-jigs round their necks.'

Then Madge, nodding kindly at the old lady, went upstairs, and, after looking into the sitting-room to tell Rose to get her dinner by herself, as she felt too tired and unwell to eat, went to her own room, and, locking the door, threw herself at full length upon her bed. There are some people upon whom any great grief has a stunning overwhelming effect, so overwhelming that it numbs their brain and paralyses their power of thought. Madge Pierrepoint was of these. With all the wish, she felt utterly powerless to deliberate what effect her recent interview with her husband ought to have on her future life, or even to recollect the details of that interview. It was all too sudden, too recent; the weight of the blow seemed to have deprived her of the power of thinking over what would be its re-sult, or even when it had been given. She strove to rally, to collect her senses, to think it over; but all in vain. She lay in a dull lethargic state, from which the recollection of what Miss Cave had said about Gerald Hardinge roused her only for an instant. Then she relapsed, and, gradually losing consciousness, fell into a deep unbroken sleep.

In that state she remained, until she was roused by a loud knocking at the door, and Rose's voice outside, telling her it was time for her to go to the theatre. At first she listened mechanically, without the power to move or even to speak, then muttering something sufficient to satisfy her sister that she had been heard, Madge struggled into a sitting position, and clasping her head with both her hands, strove to collect her scattered senses, and to comprehend what had been passing around her. It flashed upon her in an instant, the interview with Philip in the lane, the long dreary walk back, with heavy heart and wavering footsteps, the talk with Miss Cave, and her mention of the Avonmouth Theatre. She recollected it all, but what would be the result of it all was as far off as ever; she had come to no decision,

and she could come to none now. What she
had to do now was to hurry off to the theatre
and to act. To act! With the feeling of an
iron band around her temples, and her heart
throbbing like a ball of fire.

Mr. Dunsany's friends, who, as Miss Cave
expected, mustered in large numbers, were
very much pleased with their evening's entertainment, more especially when the hero of
the night came on in the after-piece, wearing,
in addition to his theatrical costume, the in-
signia of the Order of Friendly Brothers, to
which he belonged, and interpolated in his
dialogue many mystic allusions, only understood by the initiated. The audience generally was of a convivial rather than of a critical
character, and more appreciative of the comic
than of the tragic acting. It was agreed on
all sides, however, that Miss Pierrepoint was
' a fine woman,' and if she failed in impress-
ing them as they had been led to believe,
they laid it more to their own want of com-
prehension, than to any shortcoming on her
part.

As for Madge herself, she acknowledged afterwards she owed it entirely to the early training of her memory, and to her methodical practice of her profession, that she got through her part at all. She dressed herself in a dream, and in a dream she went through her various scenes, speaking when the cue was given to her, and not missing a word of what she had to say, 'doing her spouting,' as Philip Vane would have called it, with due emphasis and intonation, but with eyes that were without fire, and gesticulations void of life or energy. How she got through it she knew not, but at last her performance came to an end, and she was led on before the curtain by the delighted Dunsany. Still dazed, she went to her dressing-room, and exchanged her theatrical attire for her ordinary walking-dress. Still dazed, she was coming forth from the stage-door, when she was confronted by Gerald Hardinge, who took her hand.

Then she roused at once.

'Good - evening, Miss Pierrepoint,' said Gerald, very polite, and rather distant, for

Gonnop, the hall-keeper, was standing close by, and his ears were full-cocked; 'may I have the pleasure of seeing you home?'

Madge thanked him for his proposed escort, and they went out together.

When they were in the street, and out of hearing, Gerald turned to her and said:

'Didn't Rose give you my message?'

'Certainly.'

'And you were going away without waiting for me?'

'Not at all. I fully expected to see you where I did.'

'Did you? And yet you looked astonished as though my presence had taken you quite unawares. You have had that same strange look, however, during the whole evening. I was watching you from the wings while you were acting, and I saw it then. I see it now.'

'Do you?' said Madge, trying to smile, but there was a leaden weight on her eyelids, and the muscles of her mouth refused to move.

'Yes,' said Gerald Hardinge, gazing into

her face; 'your appearance gives me the notion of some one who has been bewitched, or
is under a spell.'

'Break the spell, then, and exorcise the
demon,' cried Madge, still striving against
herself; 'but don't let us stand here in the
middle of the street, glaring into each other's
faces, or we shall excite the wonderment of
the passers-by.'

'No,' said Gerald; 'let me take you home,
I have lots to say to you.'

'We won't go to my lodgings, I think,
Gerald,' said Madge, mindful of what Miss
Cave had said to her in the morning; 'let's
walk round the crescent, there is not a soul
near, and you shall tell me all you have to
say.'

'As you please,' he said shortly.

'Don't be angry, Gerald; I am sure I am
right in what I am doing,' whispered Madge,
laying her hand on his arm. And instantly
he was tamed and happy.

As they turned into the crescent, the
chimes of the cathedral clock rang out the

four quarters, and the deep bell struck eleven. Listening to it, and looking up at the great yellow moon riding high in the sky, Madge recollected where she had been the same hour on the previous evening, and an irrepressible shudder ran through her frame. Gerald felt the vibration of the hand lying on his arm, and looked down gravely and earnestly at her.

'What is it, Madge?' he asked. 'You trembled then from head to foot; there is something the matter with you. What is it? I insist upon knowing!'

· There is nothing wrong with me, Gerald, indeed,' said Madge; 'believe me there is not. I have been working hard, you know, and I was perhaps a little overcome by the fatigue and the heat. But the season is over now, and I shall have rest—at least until I go to Avonmouth.'

'O, Dobson has made that proposition already, has he?' said Gerald. 'I knew he was going to do so, but I scarcely thought it would be so quick; however, you are not going to Avonmouth, Madge.'

'You are not, Gerald, I know.'

'Nor are you!'

'Are my future movements, then, to be influenced by yours, sir?'

'I hope and trust so, Madge,' said the young man earnestly; 'I devoutly hope and trust so.'

There was something in his tone which had more effect in rousing her and fixing her attention than anything she had experienced within the last twenty-four hours. Up to this point she had been striving against an overpowering lassitude and want of energy, which still retained their hold upon her; had been trying to laugh and make light conversation, as it were, for the mere sake of keeping herself up to the required pitch of answering her companion's remarks. But his last few earnest words had worked a charm. Her attention was aroused, and her interest excited.

'If that is to be the case,' said she, 'you must no longer talk in riddles, but speak out plainly, Gerald.'

'I want nothing better,' said the young man. 'I told Rose, last night, to let you know I wanted to speak to you on a most important matter.'

'Yes, I recollect on making the appointment Rose told me that it was important; and it is important, is it, Gerald?'

'To me the most important matter in my life,' said Gerald, not looking at her, and speaking very low.

'Tell me, then,' said Madge, in the same tone.

Under the fascination of that moment, with his low voice murmuring in her ear, her hand resting on his arm, in the full conscious-ness that he was devoted to her body and soul, the great mental agony she had just been labouring under melted away entirely for the time.

'Tell me, then,' she whispered again.

'Why should I tell you the first part of it again?' he murmured, 'unless, indeed, you have the same gratification in hearing that I have in saying it. You know how I love and worship you, my darling! How, since the first hour I saw you, I have been your slave, never happy but when near you, and having no other thought but of and for you. You hear me, Madge?'

She made him no answer, save what he might infer from the smallest pressure of her hand upon his arm.

'I have said all this to you before, and you have listened to me and laughed at me, and while you half forbade my thus addressing you, let me go on, because you said it was idle talk. I told you then that the time would come when such talk would be idle no longer, when I might have the power of attaining such a position as would enable me to ask you to marry me. You recollect all this, Madge?'

He bent his head and looked down at her. Her face was very white, and it was more by the motion of her lips than from anything he heard, that he understood her to assent.

'Do you recollect further what you said?'
'I do.'

'I recollect the very words: " You shall ask me when the time arrives, Gerald," you said, " and I will answer you then." Madge, the time has arrived now, and I claim your answer.'

' Gerald!' said Madge, with a low cry.

' It has arrived now, my darling,' he continued, passing his arm around her. 'I am to remain a scene-painter and a theatre drudge no longer. Listen, dear one! For months past I have been working in secret, and have completed two pictures, which I sent to London. Yesterday morning I heard from the agent I had consigned them to, that they have been bought at the prices which I had fixed upon them; bought, the agent tells me, by some rich, eccentric old man, who wishes me to come to London, and pledges himself to find sufficient commissions for me to occupy my time for months to come. More than this, the agent advises me at once to come to town, and introduce myself to my patron, as, should he take a fancy to me, there is no knowing where the good results may end. When I got that letter, Madge, my first thought was of you; now, I said, I can ask her to be my wife; now I can ask her to link her lot with mine, not as the obscure drudge of a country theatre, but as one who has a fair prospect of fame and fortune; now I can offer her rest from the toil she has undergone, and freedom from the annoyances and insolences which she is compelled to put up with. Madge, darling, I can, I do, offer you this now. What do you say in reply?'

Nothing.

She said nothing. He drew her closely to him, and bending down noticed that her eyelids were closed, and when he pressed his lips upon her cheek, it was stone cold.

Gerald feared she had fainted, but immediately afterwards she half unclosed her eyes, and murmured, in broken tones, 'I am very ill, Gerald! Take me home—take me home!'

CHAPTER VIII.

IN her room at last. Unseen by Miss Cave,
who had remained at the theatre to settle
accounts with Dunsany, and to talk over the
pros and *cons* of the suggested Avonmouth
season with manager Dobson. Scarcely seen
by her sister Rose, who had been awaiting
her arrival impatiently, and who rushed forward, directly she entered, to ask her what
had been the purport of Gerald Hardinge's
communication, but whose love was greater
even than her curiosity, and who, on seeing
that Madge was ill and suffering, at once
consented to postpone her inquiries until the
morning.

In her own room at last, with the door

locked, her hot heavy clothes thrown aside, and a light dressing-gown donned in their place. There she is, seated at the dressing-table, her hair thrown back over her shoulders, and her chin resting on her hand. The time was now arrived when she could think it all out, the time that she longed for during her weary walk homeward up the Dumping-ton-road, the time that she longed for as she lay prostrate, dazed and semi-conscious, upon the bed before going to the theatre. She could think it all out now—all—all. Why, good Heavens! even since she was last in that room what a change had swept over the current of her life! What a new vista for the future had been opened up before her!

He did intend that the Australian journey should be merely an excuse for a separation, not merely temporary, but final. When she taxed him with it, he acknowledged it. She was glad she had been beforehand with him there; that was one instance, at least, where the cunning on which he so prided him-

self had not been able to cajole or deceive
her. What a moral coward he was! He would
have taken leave of her with fine promises
and pleasant speeches, and let her go away;
and then, when he knew himself to be far beyond her reach, he would have let her know
the truth, that he had deserted her and cast
her off for ever. Not even then, perhaps: he
might have allowed her to go on wearing away
her life, hoping against hope, and ignorant of
the state of widowhood to which she had long
since been abandoned.

Now she knew the worst. Come what
might in the future, at least she would not
drift into it unprepared. He had spoken
plainly enough, said in so many words, that
marriage was dissolved between them. He
must have had that step in contemplation for
some time past; such a resolution was not
taken on the spur of the moment. And as
she passed in review the recent occasions on
which she and Philip Vane had met, and the
tone of the few short letters he had written
to her, she saw clearly how he had, bit by

bit, been loosening the tie—never very strong, save in its legality—which existed between them, and preparing for the final rupture.

And now it had come. 'You will never look upon my face again;' that was what he said. What had she done? Had she been so specially wicked, had her life been so specially happy, that she should be visited by an affliction like this, that she should be forced to bear the brunt of the battle alone, quite unaided; more than that, even having to succour and provide for one weaker and younger than herself, without one friend to turn to in her extremity, without one living soul to speak to her a kind word, or to lend her a helping hand?

Gerald Hardinge! As the thought flashed across her the name rose simultaneously to her lips, and was spoken aloud.

She raised her face from her hands, where in the agony of her grief she had buried it, and catching sight of its reflection in the glass before her, could not help noticing, all blurred and tear-stained as it was,

the delicacy of its features, the sweetness of
its expression. She peered at it long and
curiously, as though it had been another woman's face, now pitting a dimple with her
finger, now tracing with her nail the track of
a line or two which had already begun to appear near her eyes. Then suddenly pushing
her chair aside she rose to her feet and again
muttered aloud, 'Gerald Hardinge!'

'The last time that Gerald spoke to me,'
she continued, pacing to and fro in the room,
'I listened to him carelessly and talked to
him lightly. Knowing the barrier that existed
between us, there was no harm, I thought, in
so listening, for it was a break in my dull and
dreary life, and a pastime to me; and I knew
that Gerald was too much of a gentleman to
say anything that might not properly be said
to—what he imagined me to be—a good and
virtuous girl. Now that barrier exists no
longer, and he must learn the truth; I must
tell him that I am the deserted wife of another man, that the confidence and companionship which have hitherto existed between us

must now be brought to an end, that the terms
on which we have hitherto lived, were they to
continue, would be dangerous to him and
compromising for me. Yes,' she added, after
a pause, during which she had remained rapt
in consideration, 'the retribution which Philip
Vane will inflict upon me for refusing to obey
his commands will be bitter indeed. He can
disappear, " efface himself," as he says, banish
all remembrance of me, if it be not already
banished, blot out all traces of his married
life, commence a fresh career of dissipation,
and look for a new victim to wheedle, and
make use of, and desert. He can do all this,
for he will be free, while I must remain here,
fettered and heart-broken and solitary.'

She flung herself prone upon the bed, and
clasping her hands behind her head, lay there
motionless for some time. When at length
she raised her face from the pillow in which
it had been hidden, there was on it a strange
odd expression, such as those who were most
intimate with it had never seen there. A
bright scarlet patch burned on each of her

cheeks, there was a wild restless look in her large brown eyes, and her lips, ordinarily so soft and mobile, were set and rigid.

'Why should I be solitary?' she broke forth, raising herself on her elbow, and gazing eagerly before her. 'Why should his be all the triumph, and mine all the misery? Why, while he creates a fresh life for himself, should I settle down in apathetic wretchedness and dull despair? He said, truly enough, that our secret was our own, that our marriage was known to none but ourselves; and that when he decided upon ignoring it, it would be just as though it had never happened. It was known but to ourselves and to two others, hired witnesses, whom in no human probability I shall ever come across. What is to prevent me, then, from shaking myself free from the shackles, and seeing whether in life there is not yet some happiness in store for me? What is to prevent? My conscience? Duty? The duty I owe to Philip Vane would sit lightly enough upon me; and is it not his wish? " I will never interfere with your plans and pro-

jects, be they what they may;" he swore that,
and he will keep his word, only too thankful
to lay hold of any act of mine which would
tend to our farther estrangement and ratify
the separation between us.

'And here is Gerald, whose only thought
is to take me to his heart, and make me his
wife, who, hard worked as he is at the theatre,
has been devoting his extra hours in labour
to gain a position which he could consider
worthy to offer me, and who is steeped to the
lips not merely in patient devotion to me, but
in the desire to rid me of the burden which I
now have to bear, and to render life smooth
and easy to me.

'Gerald Hardinge's wife! He asked me
to become so at once, why should I refuse?
I am older than he is, it is true, and my youth
has been passed in toil, and, to a certain ex-
tent, in privation. But,' she added, stopping
before the glass, and again surveying her features in it, 'I do not think I show the traces
of it; I do not think, speaking dispassionately,
as Heaven knows I feel, there are many who

are better or more attractive-looking, however much my beauty may have palled on Philip Vane.

'Gerald Hardinge's wife! Could I return the love he gives me? My capabilities of loving have not been put to any severe test; it was that silly admiration of a good-looking face and specious manners which led me to like Philip Vane; the idiotic folly of a schoolgirl, which raves about the colour of a man's eyes, or the shape of his nose; but I doubt whether there was much question of love in the matter. I was sillily fascinated by him in the first few days of our married life; I remember I showed it as much as he would let me, but that is so far off that it seems like a dream. Since then I have been almost constantly separated from him; and when we have met there has been no question of love between us, certainly none shown, even of regard, on his part. I wonder whether I have ever possessed the faculty of loving, and if so, whether it has died out? I think I can answer that question,' she said, smiling gravely.

' Last night, when Gerald's arm was round me holding me closely to him, when his face was bending close to mine, when I felt his soft breath on my cheek, and saw the lovelight trembling and fading in his eyes, a shiver ran through me from head to foot, and my soul yearned towards him with a passion hitherto strange to it. Ah, why,' she cried, clasping her hands above her head, 'why should my life be solitary and blank? Why should this wealth of love which I possess be thus wasted? Why should I not solace what remains to me of my youth, and give up such beauty as I still possess to him who prizes it so dearly? I cannot, I will not, let slip this chance which is offered me so opportunely. I will write a line to Gerald telling him that I accept his offer, and am only impatient to call myself his wife. and thus at the same time I will gratify my love for him, and my revenge on Philip Vane.'

The scarlet spot on her cheek burned more brightly than before, and the light was still in her eyes; but the muscles of her mouth,

instead of being rigid and set, were moving involuntarily, and her lips were full and humid.

She took her blotting-book and ink-stand
from off the chest of drawers, arranged them
on the table, and sat down to write. But her
brain was too much excited, her heart beating
far too quickly, to admit of her sufficiently
steadying her thoughts; and the next moment she was up and pacing the room again
to and fro, to and fro. No reminiscences of
past misery now; all visions of future happiness with Gerald! How handsome he was!
how high-bred and gentlemanly he always
looked! Not even his coarse common paint-
ing-clothes could disfigure him. How softly
he always spoke to her, and how he always
looked straight into her eyes—not boldly, not
triumphantly, but with a strange mixture of
diffidence and love! She recollected too the
long clinging pressure of his hand. Ah, how
she would love him, how she would make up
for past years of coldness and neglect! She
longed to have him there by her side, that
she might tell him how warmly she recipro-

cated all he had said to her on the previous
night. Unable to see him at that instant, she
must write to him; that was the next best
thing she could do, and she would do so at
once.

Seated at the table once again, one hand
drumming on the blotting-book, the other
idly stretched on the paper in front of her.
How should she commence her letter to him?
How should she end it? She knew that, she
thought. She should put 'your wife.' His
wife? And then the pen slipped from between
her fingers, and the other hand ceased drumming, and convulsively grasped the table.

His wife? Not his, but Philip Vane's.

That fact remained indisputable, notwithstanding Philip's repudiation of it, and in spite
of all the sophistry which he had talked, and
which she had allowed herself to be persuaded
into accepting. Philip Vane's wife, in the
sight of heaven, and in the eye of the law.
Philip Vane's wife—that was her condition,
only to be released therefrom by her own or
his death.

Ah, what vague hopes she had cherished
of placing herself on an equality with him!
what fruitless boasts she had made to herself
of claiming as much freedom in her future as
he had insisted on his! Were she to take the
step she had contemplated—were she to accept the position offered to her—the mere
prospect of the expectation of which had filled
her with happiness and joy inexplicable—what
would be the result? In her own secret soul
she would know herself, whatever she might
pass for to him and to the world, not to be Gerald Hardinge's wife, but his mistress, and to be
Philip Vane's wife still. Even if—looking at
the happiness which such a prospect opened
up to her, and contrasting it with the certain
misery of her future — misery embittered a
thousandfold by the omnipresent recollection
of what might have been — she could have
stifled the voice of conscience, and clung to
the chance thus offered, what guarantee had
she that Philip Vane might not some day or
other put in an appearance upon the scene,
and seek to gain advantage by her default?

He had sworn that he would not do so; but she knew well enough that to such a man such an oath meant nothing; and then for the mere passing gratification of two passions, revenge and love, she would have entailed misery not merely upon herself, but upon the boy who had offered his life for her disposal, and so frankly and loyally had placed his future in her hands.

Following out with strictest scrutiny her self-examination, Madge felt compelled to confess that there were several reasons for giving up the step on which she had so recently determined. The difference of age between them must not be lost sight of. It was well enough now, while Gerald was under the influence of his boyish passion, and while she yet retained enough of her youthful beauty to keep him in thrall, and to render her an object of admiration among his friends. But in a few, very few years' time, she would have lost her bloom, and be advancing towards middle age, while he would yet be in the prime of early manhood. What should she expect then but what

she had already undergone? Not that it was
possible Gerald could ever treat her as Philip
Vane had treated her—he was too manly, too
high-spirited, too tender-hearted; but would
it not be worse for her than anything she had
yet endured, to see that she was merely toler-
ated by a man to whom her whole soul was
given, and in whom the wild ardour of love
had been superseded by a feeling of mere ten-
derness and compassion?

No, no—a thousand times no! She could
bear anything but that. Better pluck out this
passion of recent growth, though she plucked
out her heart and her life at the same time,
than let it have a short season of bloom,
and a long period of withering decay. The
mirage was fast vanishing away, and again the
long level sands of the desert of life which she
was compelled to travel, with no well of hope,
no oasis of rest and happiness in sight, lay
stretching out before her. The shining sands
had to be traversed, and the bubbling foun-
tains and the palm-trees' shade had proved
mere mockeries of mental vision; so let her

proceed upon her pilgrimage at once, and give up all farther thought of those unsubstantial and impossible delights. It could not, must not be. And when Madge Pierrepoint had once faced that fact, although in facing it she went through such mental torture as, since the world's creation, has been suffered only by those white-robed few who sacrifice their all in all for duty's sake, she determined on carrying out her resolutions, and came out of the conflict worn and pale and haggard, indeed, but victorious and determined.

What was to be done? The proper course for her to pursue was, as she knew, to see Gerald, and tell him all. But that she could not do. She dared not trust herself. Her courage was insufficient, not merely to carry her through the story of her wrongs, but to bear her up in what she knew to be the unavoidable result, his appeal to her to throw her past life to the winds, and intrust him with her future. She dared not trust herself to see him again; she must hurry away from that place, within the next few hours, in the

early morning, and leave what she had to say
to him in a note which would be given to Miss
Cave. What should she say in that note?
Tell him the real state of the case, and appeal
to his sense of honour, to his feeling of pity,
not to attempt to follow her? That would
never do. Madge Pierrepoint's experience of
the world was not large; but it was sufficient
to tell her that when a man, and especially
a young man, is madly in love, appeals to
such sentiments are generally made in vain.
Such a confession would probably act as a
provocative to his pursuit, and that must be
stopped at any cost. Seeing Gerald under
such circumstances as those, Madge would not
have answered for herself; and all the mental
anguish which she had undergone, and the
triumph which she had obtained, would have
been in vain.

After reflection, then, she came to the conclusion that there was but one way by which
the end she sought for was to be obtained.

And that way was, to strike his kind and
trusting heart a blow which, coming from her

hand, would numb and paralyse its action, and
prevent its ever again throbbing in response
to hers. She 'must be cruel only to be kind,'
and must be content to pass as cold and heart-
less in Gerald's eyes, rather than let him know
her for what she really was. Knowing Gerald
as Madge did, she never doubted for an instant that he would refuse to take from her lips
any denial which was dictated by prudence or
policy, and that the only method by which he
could be restrained from farther pursuit would
be by touching his pride. That must be done,
no matter at what cost to herself; wittingly
and knowingly, she must degrade herself in
the sight of the man who so loved her, and
had just asked permission to dedicate his life
to her.

So she sat down to do it. There, spread
out before her, lay the paper which was to
have borne his summons to her side, whereon
was to have been written her acceptance of
his offer. She thought of all this, and the
pen which she had taken up dropped again
from her fingers. Ah, surely the task was

too cruel, the self-imposed burden too heavy
for her to bear! Was it not too much to
expect that she should not merely continue
in the strait and thorny path, closing her
eyes to the temptations of the lovely gardens
stretching on either side of her, but that she
should be called upon to wound and outrage
him who offered to share that paradise with
her? She could not do it — she could not
do it! And Madge hid her face in her hands,
and the bitter tears burst forth again. When
the paroxysm was over, she rose and bathed
her face, and once more returned to the table.
Then, stopping for some time to try and get
more command over her trembling fingers, to
try and still the audible beating of her heart,
to try and find words in which her meaning
might be, with as little harshness as possible,
expressed, she wrote the following letter:

'My DEAR GERALD, — If you have ever
had any kind feeling for me, and I know
you have, Gerald, you will need to remember
it all when you read this. What I write now

I ought to have said to you last night, if not
before. No, not before, for up till last night
I had only looked upon what you have said
to me from time to time as so much boyish
nonsense, not to be thought of seriously by
either of us. I knew that most boys—don't
be offended, Gerald, there will come a time
when you will consider youth a thing not to
be ashamed of—that most boys admire women older than themselves; and there was
a greater reason for your liking me, as we
have been thrown so much together, and
there are not many people—in the company,
at least, I mean — with whom you seem to
have much in common. I have always, as
you will remember, Gerald, endeavoured to
stop you when you were going to say anything definite to me; I have always refused
to give you any definite answer, on the plea
that it would be sufficient to ask me for one
when you were in a position to speak seriously to me. Last night you told me that
time had now arrived, and it is my duty
therefore to speak definitely to you.

'Gerald, I cannot be your wife! I must
not even be to you what I have been — a
chosen companion, a woman in whose society
you have been happy! In saying this I am
not hard nor worldly. I have no doubt of
your success in life, and I know that, should
you continue to think as you do at present,
your pleasure in that success would be doubled
if it were shared by me. Should you continue to think? Ah, that is one point, Gerald!
You have not seen enough of the world to
know your own mind, and the woman whom
you worship now might seem very homely
and very dull to you in a few years' time!

'But my chief reason for writing to you
is to tell you that I am no longer free, that
I have for some time been engaged to be
married to a gentleman who now claims my
promise. I ought to have told you this last
night, Gerald, but I was overcome by the
extra fatigue which I had undergone during
the past week, and my dread of the annoy-
ance which I knew my answer would give
you was too much for me, so I write it to

you instead! You must try and not think
very badly of me for not telling you before.
I had my reasons, reasons which I cannot
explain now, but may be able to do so some
day. I am going away from this at once,
and am to be married very shortly. Good-
bye, Gerald! God bless you! Most likely
we shall never meet again, but I shall always
think gratefully of the kindness that you
have shown to me, and pray for your welfare.
Once more, good-bye!

'Yours sincerely,

'MARGARET PIERREPOINT.'

It was finished at last, after many alterations and much delay. As Madge read it
over she said to herself, 'This is doing evil
that good may come of it; may God forgive
me this bitter, bitter lie!' Then she folded
the letter, addressed it, shut it in her blotting-
book, and went into Rose's bedroom.

The sun had risen by this time and was
pouring in through the thin white curtains.
Madge stepped softly up to the bed, and could

not help noticing Rose's delicate beauty as she lay with her face upturned and her head resting on one of her arms.

'Too delicate and too sensitive to do much in the great battle of life,' said Madge as she bent over her. 'Poor little flower, it's lucky she has me to stand between her and the rough wind outside. Smiling in her sleep, too,' she added, after a moment's pause; 'it seems a shame to rouse her from a pleasant dream to the dull realities of packing and departure, but the time grows short, and we have much to do.'

Then she touched her sister lightly on the shoulder, and the girl awoke and sat up in bed, looking before her with large eyes full of surprise.

'What is it, Madge?' she cried. 'What has made you awake so early? I am generally up long before you; and your eyelids are all red and swollen too. I don't believe you have been to bed all night. What is the matter?'

'No, dear,' said the elder sister quietly,

'there is nothing the matter, only you must get up at once and pack your own things, and help me to pack mine; we are going away.'

'Going away!' repeated Rose. 'When?'

'Now directly, by the seven o'clock train. We have scarcely time for our packing and our breakfast.'

'But where are we going to, Madge, and why?'

'I don't know yet, dear, where, though probably we shall stop first at Springside; and as for why, Rose, the answer is, because I wish it.'

Then Rose, who knew that when her sister was in what she was pleased to call 'one of those tempers' there was no gainsaying her, promised to get up immediately, and Madge returned to her room, and began emptying her chest of drawers of its contents.

As she was in the midst of her packing, Miss Cave, who had been roused by the dragging about of the boxes, came in full of wonder and surprise at all she saw and heard. For Madge told the old lady a long story

about her being not merely much fatigued,
but more seriously out of health than she had
imagined, adding, that Doctor Kent, whom
she had consulted, had recommended her to
try the mineral waters at Springside, and that
she was about to proceed there with that object.

It was a great blow to Miss Cave to lose
sight of her favourite, even for, as she ima.
gined, a very short period, as she had fully
calculated on their being together at Avonmouth. However, as the old lady remarked,
an extra pound a week and half a clear benefit
were good things in their way, but not to
be compared to health, and Doctor Kent's
opinion should be followed to the letter.

The packing was completed, the preparations for departure were all made, and they
were standing on the platform just before the
train started, when Madge handed to Miss
Cave a letter, and requested that it might
be sent round to Mr. Hardinge's lodging.
Her hand did not tremble in the slightest
degree, nor was there in her face, which was

closely scanned by the old lady, a trace of any unusual expression. Once resolved that the sacrifice was due from her, Madge went to the stake not merely with courage but with dignity.

CHAPTER IX.

DOUBT.

WHEN Gerald Hardinge saw the street-door close, shutting Madge Pierrepoint from his view, he remained stationary for a minute, gazing on the spot whence she had disappeared, and then turned away with an indescribable feeling of happiness and elation in his breast. Her last words to him had been but feebly uttered, it is true, and had told him that she was ill, but he believed this illness to be merely the result of mental excitement and physical prostration, which would speedily pass away, never to reappear in the calm happy future which he had planned for her, while the thrilling pressure of her hand, as she left him, gave higher hopes than could be given by any words that this future was accepted by her.

As the young man walked with a light quick step along the deserted streets, he lifted his hat to catch as much as possible of the cool night breeze, which retained some of the freshness of the sea, whence it was blown, mingled with the fragrance of the gardens and orchards which it had traversed in its career towards the old city, and raising his eyes to the star-strewn blue heavens above him, felt half inclined to believe that all nature gloried in his happiness, and shared in his success. Conscious presently of the creeping, shambling female figure by his side, which addressed him in whining tones, imploring alms, he stopped and handed to it such largess as to evoke a shower of fulsome thanks from its recipient, who hurried away, fearful lest a second thought should make him repent of his munificence. Needless to say that no such thought crossed Gerald's mind. Not on such a night as that at least could he be appealed to in vain; he had him-

self been made supremely happy, and only
delighted in doing what he could to increase
the happiness of others.

Supremely happy indeed! The silence of
the streets was almost oppressive to him.
He wanted to take not man but nature into
his confidence. He wanted to be alone in a
garden, on a mountain top, in a boat upon
the river or the sea, anywhere, so that without rendering himself ridiculous he could put
into words the gratitude that filled his heart,
the joy that thrilled his frame, and tingled
in his pulses. Even there, in the Precinct,
hemmed in by the high old gabled houses,
inside of which the decorous dignitaries of
the cathedral and their staid families lay
wrapped in dreamless slumber, he felt inclined to cry aloud, to break into a swift
running pace, to do anything which would
give vent to the unspoken joy then pent
within his breast.

It was lucky that he refrained from giving
way to any of these eccentricities; for the
next moment, as he turned the corner of

the street, he found himself confronted by a group of men who were advancing from the opposite direction. Scarcely gazing at them—assuredly not recognising any of them —Gerald was stepping into the roadway with the intention of allowing them to pass, when he heard his own name called out in a loud tone, and immediately recognised the voice pronouncing it as belonging to Mr. Dunsany. The speaker was indeed that histrionic genius, who followed up his salutation by seizing Gerald lightly by the collar, and, as he turned round to his admiring friends, calling out with tragic emphasis, 'Trapped at last.'

'Trapped at last,' echoed a tall man, with a thin hatchet face, bright beady eyes, and a thick moustache. 'Deuced good title for a three-act drama; see my way to it at once. Act the first, Setting the Snare; act the second, Knotting the Noose; act the third, Trapped at Last. Lapse of ten years is supposed to occur between the second and third acts. There you have it!'

'O, drop that gaff, Hayward,' said Dunsany; 'and you, Gerald, don't stand there looking like old Blowhard when he plays the Idiot Witness.'

'A part which comes quite natural to him,' interrupted Mr. Hayward.

'Well, come along, Gerald,' continued Dunsany; 'we have got a little supper at the Swan, and I have been looking everywhere for you to make one of the party. Now I've got you, so come along.'

'Not to-night,' commenced Gerald; 'I am awfully tired, and was on my way home to bed. Not to-night, please.'

'O, no, not to-night,' repeated Dunsany in a bantering tone, 'certainly not to-night; let us say we will meet this night twelve-month, and at Philippi, please! Come out of that, you villain! Do you think I am going to let you go now I have once got hold of you? More especially when old Blowhard told me just now you were not coming back to him, and he should have to look out for a new scene-painter. Put your arm in mine, and come along.'

'But I really am horribly tired,' pleaded Gerald.

'If you are tired, Count' (the nickname which Gerald Hardinge's looks and manners had gained for him amongst the company, and by which he generally went), 'if you are tired, Count,' said another of the by-standers, Mr. Minneken, a dashing young *roué* of fifty-eight, with a purple head and a ragged purple moustache, and who was the light comedian of the company, 'go to your bed at the natural hour of four A.M. Never invoke the miserable Morpheus at a time which should be sacred to the blisses of Bacchus and the kisses of Venus.'

A general chorus of 'Bravo, Minny!' rewarded this flight of fancy.

'Letting alone the fact that I sleep next to you, my dear Gerald,' said Dunsany, 'and that when I arrive at the hour so neatly indicated just now, I am likely to disturb you from your slumber.'

The proposition to end his evening in this manner was assuredly very different from what Gerald Hardinge had either expected or wished. He had longed for some place in which he could commune with himself, for some solitude where he could orally convince himself of the happiness which he had just secured; and he was now bidden to make one of a party of convivial roisterers in a tavern reeking with liquor and tobacco. But he did not like to urge any farther the refusal to the invitation thus pressed upon him. Several of those present, and especially Dunsany, had shown him much rough kindness and attention during the time he had passed among them, and he was conscious that there was prevalent in the company an intuitive suspicion of the difference between his former and his present position in life, which would render them doubly susceptible to any apparent slight. So he ceased to make any farther opposition to their wishes, and his assent being received with a shout which awoke the slumbering echoes of the old Guildhall portico, and brought the policeman down a by-street with hurried foot-steps very dif-

ferent from his usual measured pace, the party
proceeded on their way rejoicing.

The Swan, towards which the convivial
company was making its way, was a regular
type of a theatrical tavern. Ordinarily, the
house 'used' by the actors and their friends
is to be found in the immediate vicinity of
the theatre. But the inhabitants of Wexeter
had scruples about allowing any establishment of the kind to flourish in the proximity
of the cathedral; while the church dignitaries,
who were potential in such matters, took care
that the precincts dwelt in by them should
be kept free from the contamination of a
tavern of any kind, and especially one which
was likely to be frequented by the lower class
of theatrical performers. So that the Swan
was compelled to build her nest at some little
distance off, down at the bottom of the hill
indeed, and near the wharves abutting on the
navigable portion of the river Wexe, where
huge balks of timber lie strewn about, where
the road is always gritty with coal-dust, and
where there is a perpetual maritime smell

of boiling pitch and fresh tar. None of the
bargemen, Jacks-in-the-water, or river-side
idlers, however, dream of going into the
Swan, which is known as the actors' house
of call, and is given up exclusively to them.
The landlord is a retired 'heavy man' from
the Norfolk circuit; his wife, stout and un-
wieldy though she be now, was once the
brightest of singing chambermaids at Ports-
mouth; and his two sons, with their celebrated dog Beppo, are now extracting money
from the pockets of Australian diggers, by
their splendid performance of the *Forest of
Bondy*. All day long, lounging in front of
the street-door, or leaning listlessly against
the portal, are to be seen sallow, keen-eyed
men, whiskerless, indeed, but with an outline blue map on cheek and chin, showing
what tremendous hirsute power is kept in
abeyance by the exigences of the profession.
From time to time they will enter the house
and drop into the bar—a snuggery where not
one scrap of wall is to be seen, so covered is
it with play-bills and placards, and portraits

of celebrated theatrical characters — take a drink standing, chat with the barmaid, who, like every other inmate of the establishment, is steeped to the lips in dramatic lore, or glance through the pages of the *Haresfoot*, the theatrical journal, especially conning the advertisements of managers in quest of talent.

In the course of the theatrical season many banquets were usually given at the Swan, actors being proverbially of a hospitable and generous disposition; and no success of even the smallest kind was ever gained by any member of the company without its being duly commemorated in liquor. But there was never any noise or disturbance at these entertainments; and as the house was thoroughly well conducted, the police never interfered with its arrangements, and winked at occasional infractions of the law which prescribed a certain hour for closing.

That hour had pretty nearly arrived when Mr. Dunsany and his friends reached the Swan; and most of the ordinary guests had taken their departure. For the expected party,

however, a room was prepared; and in a few
minutes they were all seated round the table
covered with the materials for a substantial
meal. As the host, Mr. Dunsany took the
chair, having Gerald on his right, and Mr.
Minneken on his left. They were all too
hungry to talk much at first; and, when their
appetite began to be appeased, the conversation which ensued was such as might be expected in such a circle. The performances
of the evening and of the past season generally, the shortcomings, meannesses, and vanity
of the manager Dobson (always spoken of as
Blowhard), the chances of London engagements, and the gratitude due to the press, of
which Mr. Hayward was the esteemed representative then present. All these subjects
were in turn discussed; and Gerald, who had
taken very little part in the conversation,
thought he saw the longed-for opportunity
to slip away unperceived, when he heard a
remark which instantly changed his intention.

Mr. Minneken was the speaker.

'A divinity, sir,' he exclaimed; 'Madge Pierrepoint is a divinity, nothing else. There is nothing to touch her on the stage nowadays, nor has there been in my time. I've seen them all, sir—the finest women in London, by George! and there is not one of them you can compare to our Madge. Such an arched neck, such pouting lips, such a mass of capillary attractions, such a magnificent mane. By heavens, sir, she is delicious!' And Mr. Minneken first kissed the tips of his fingers, and then waved them in the air.

When Gerald first heard the name of the woman he loved thus mentioned in a public company, he felt hot and angry. But it was impossible to be annoyed with Mr. Minneken, so earnest and impulsive was he, so chivalrous, and withal so respectful. Gerald recollected, moreover, that he had heard Madge speak of the kindness—which it was impossible to think of as influenced by any ulterior motive—shown to her by the old beau on her first joining the company. But he feared that the subject might be taken up by others, who would not handle it quite so tenderly; and he was right.

'She is all very well to look at,' said Mr. Hayward; 'what you call a fine woman, and that sort of thing; but she's no actress.'

'No actress!' cried Dunsany.

'When did you find that out, Hayward?' asked Minneken.

'Ever since she refused to play the heroine in Hayward's five-act tragedy of *Boadicea*,' said Gerald Hardinge. 'Our friend has had no opinion of Miss Pierrepoint's talent since then.'

'Has Hayward written a five-act tragedy?' asked some one from the end of the table.

'I vote he stands a dinner, and reads it to us before it,' said Mr. Potts the prompter, who had been steadily eating ever since he arrived, and whose first utterance had reference to future food.

'No, no; after, after,' cried Dunsany. 'If he read the tragedy first, none of us would be alive for the dinner.'

'Who was Boadicea?' asked Mr. Potts's neighbour.

'Some Roman cove, I think,' said the prompter.

'It sounds to me like a name in the Bible,' said his neighbour.

'Can't say,' said Mr. Potts, whose Biblical lore was limited.

'Well, I daresay you think all this is devilish funny,' said Mr. Hayward, whose naturally sallow complexion seemed to be growing into a bright green; 'but with all deference to that very excellent young gentleman over there, I repeat my opinion that Miss Pierrepoint is no actress.'

'By heavens, sir, how you can say that I cannot understand!' said Minneken, wisely stepping in to intercept the outbreak of wrath which he anticipated from Gerald Hardinge. 'Don't even the benighted clodhoppers in this semi - agricultural, semi - ecclesiastical neighbourhood worship her? Don't they start at the smallest scintilla emitted by her glorious eye? Don't they follow every murmur of that deliciously soft voice, which comes to them through those rows of pearls like the

sighing of the west wind over a summer sea?
What more would you have, sir?'

'What more?' said Mr. Hayward savagely.
'I would have a little more go; a little more
life; a little more passion. You, Minneken,
have a reputation of having seen a good deal
of life, and you have lived long enough, heaven knows! but did you, in your experience,
ever see a woman so cold and statuesque and
passionless? Take her from first to last in
all the love-scenes she plays, and tell me is
there a scrap of heart, a scrap of warmth in
one of them?'

Before Mr. Minneken could reply, a little
man, sitting midway down the table, said,
with a low chuckling laugh:

'Perhaps she keeps her heart, and her
warmth, and her passion, and all that, for
private use. Don't do to parade 'em in public
—O, no!'

The speaker was Mr. Snick, who was the
'second old man' of the company, and who
was generally regarded as having been allotted
in life the same line of character which he had

sustained all along in the theatre, namely, being sent on to make play for others, and only
speaking in order to give other people the
chance of reply. The expression by him of
any original idea would have astonished the
company; but such an opinion, emphasised as
it was by him with his chuckle, caused intense
surprise; and a short silence ensued, which
was broken by Gerald Hardinge, who inquired,
in rather a savage tone, what grounds Mr.
Snick had for his statement.

To find the old man's remark taken seriously, delighted the company in general; and
Mr. Potts's neighbour, who had made the inquiry about Boadicea, rising to his feet, said
gravely, 'That he thought their friends would
agree with him that no gentleman had a right
to ask any questions about Mr. Snick's little
love-affairs.'

The applause and laughter which greeted
this remark incensed Gerald Hardinge still
farther. His cheeks flushed and his eyes
sparkled as he rose from his chair, and said
hurriedly:

'I care nothing about Mr. Snick, or his love-affairs either; but he alluded to a lady, whose acquaintance I have the pleasure of possessing, in an offensive way, and with a certain innuendo in his manner which I think demands explanation.'

Some of the company cried 'Hear!' some, 'Bosh!' and Mr. Dunsany called out, at the top of his voice, 'Come, Snick, you innuendoing vagabond, make a clean breast of it, and explain!'

Mr. Snick did not seem in the smallest degree put out by the hubbub and excitement he had created. On the contrary, he sat quietly sucking away at his long pipe; and when thus directly appealed to by Mr. Dunsany, he indulged in a few more chuckles before he remarked:

'What I said I will stick to. Only when I spoke before I said perhaps she kept her warmth and her passion for private use; now I say there is no perhaps at all about it—I am sure she does.'

'Sure! How the devil can you be sure?'

asked Mr. Hayward, looking across at him with a glance in which surprise was mingled with contempt.

'How can I be sure?' said the little man, with another chuckle. 'Why, from what you call in your newspaper language ocular demonstration. I have seen her.'

'Seen your grandmother!' roared out Mr. Dunsany, not liking the expression on Gerald Hardinge's face, and wishing to put an end to the discussion as quickly as possible. 'Come out of that, Snick, and don't let's have any of your anecdotes!'

'Not at all!' cried out Gerald Hardinge, starting to his feet. 'Mr. Snick, coming out of the region of possibility, has now made a positive statement respecting Miss Pierrepoint, and I demand that he now enters fully into detail concerning what he alleges he saw.'

'What right have you to demand anything of the kind?' asked Mr. Hayward.

'I will answer that question by and by,' said Gerald Hardinge very quietly.

'O, sit down, Gerald, and don't be bother-

ing about an old omadhoun like that Snick,'
said Mr. Dunsany. ' Sure, in addition to being always moithered, he has got about a pint
of punch under his belt now, and is half drunk
already!'

But Gerald Hardinge was deaf to all such
entreaty; the accusation, he said, had been
made, and must be given in detail. The
others, by degrees, came round to this opinion, and even Mr. Dunsany said, in a half-
jocular, half-savage manner :

' Come, Snick, down on your marrow-
bones, and confess your peccadillo, and I'll
promise you absolution.'

The various stages of these proceedings
seemed fraught with the greatest delight to
Mr. Snick, who still sat calmly sucking at
his pipe, and chuckling after the emission of
every separate whiff; and when he was at
length called upon to speak, he spoke slowly
and deliberately, but without the smallest
hesitation.

' Some of you may know,' he said, ' and
some mayn't, that owing to the screw I get

from old Blowhard not being too magnificent,
I endeavour to earn a little money by acting
as agent for the sale of mineral waters and
ginger-beer. There may be some among the
company present,' said the little man, looking
round him with a leer and a chuckle, ' who
may have had soda-water from me which
they have not paid for, and there may not.
But that's neither here nor there. What I
am coming to is this, that a few nights ago,
it might be, I cannot say the exact day,
but you will recollect it by that tremendous
thunder-storm which we had, the only one
there has been this summer, I thought to
myself that, not being in the bill that night,
I would just walk up as far as Dumpington
turnpike, where the tollman owed me a small
account for ginger-beer, which he manages to
sell a good deal of, it being good stuff, and
not like the penny bottles, all pop and froth.
Accordingly, soon after it was dusk, I strolled
out there, and smoked a pipe with the tollman, and got the money from him, and set
off to come back. I hadn't gone a hundred

yards before I saw—it was a dark night, but I've got eyes like a cat—I saw a tall woman coming towards me, and I recognised her figure in a minute as Miss Pierrepoint. "What are you doing here, my lady, at this time of night?" says I to myself. "I may as well see," I says to myself, and with that I slipped into the hedge. She passed me so close that her dress almost brushed against me, and then I set out after her. She went along the road, and passed the turnpike, and up that narrow lane, which, as some of you may know, runs by it. There she waited, walking up and down, as though expecting some one. I had hidden myself in another hedge, and was looking on, and presently I heard a heavy footstep, and I saw a tall man approaching. She walked straight up to meet him, and he stooped down, and put his arms around her, and kissed her. That's what he did!"

And having made his point, the little man looked round to see the result.

Mr. Snick had expected, on reaching his

climax, he would have been hailed with a shout of delight from his audience, but there was no such outburst. On the contrary, a feeling of awkwardness seemed to prevail among them, and, after looking stealthily at each other, they, with one accord, glanced towards Gerald Hardinge. The expression on Mr. Dunsany's face was especially anxious, and when Mr. Snick stopped speaking, Gerald felt his knee clasped by his friend's hand, in protest against any outbreak on his part.

The young man, however, needed no such warning. His lips twitched a little when Mr. Snick made his point, but all sign of emotion had passed away as he asked:

'The night was dark, and I think you say you did not recognise the gentleman's face?'

'No,' said Mr. Snick; 'I could only see that he was a tall man.'

'The darkness must have deceived you in that respect too,' said Gerald, with an attempt at a smile, 'for,' turning to the company, 'I cannot be considered tall, and yet I was the man who met Miss Pierrepoint on the night

in question, when this estimable gentleman
was good enough to play the spy upon our
actions.'

' You!' cried Mr. Snick.

' You!' cried Mr. Hayward.

' You!' echoed Mr. Potts the prompter.
' You been kissing and making love to our
leading lady?'

' Yes,' said Gerald Hardinge; ' yes, Mr.
Potts, and making love to her successfully, I
am happy to say, for Miss Pierrepoint is now
my affianced wife.'

CHAPTER X.

DESPAIR.

THE silence which fell upon the company at Gerald Hardinge's unexpected announcement was broken by Mr. Dunsany, who called out in his most melodious tones:

'My dear Gerald, I am delighted that you have thought the time has arrived when it is expedient to make this announcement, to the public as it were. When, weeks ago, you first mentioned to me, as your intimate friend, the fact of your engagement with Miss Pierre-point, I told you, if you recollect, that it would be advisable to make your friends ac-quainted, as speedily as possible, with the exact position of affairs, in order that there might be no possible misunderstanding. And you will acknowledge I was right, for I am sure if our friend Hayward had known how matters had stood he would not have hinted a doubt as to Miss Pierrepoint's ability; while as to Snick—'

'I beg your pardon, Dunsany,' said Mr. Hayward, 'I said nothing about Miss Pierrepoint's appearance or conduct, of both of which I have the highest admiration; but I cannot allow that even the great fact of her marrying the Count here is likely to endow her with ability, or to render her a modern Mrs. Siddons.'

'Perhaps it will be advisable to change the subject,' said Gerald Hardinge haughtily. 'After the announcement that I have made, it is perhaps scarcely in good taste to discuss Miss Pierrepoint's qualities or qualifications in my presence. The restriction, however' need be but very temporary, as I am about to take my departure; the season is broken up,' continued he, rising from his chair, 'and this will be the last time of our meeting; but I hope at some future period, gentlemen, to renew the pleasant impressions which I have had during my companionship with you, and to come amongst you once again.'

'And bring your wife,' suggested Mr. Snick, who, since the conclusion of his story, had remained perfectly quiet, sucking away at his pipe with great enjoyment.

'And bring my wife, sir!' echoed Gerald angrily. He would have said more, but for the warning pressure of Dunsany's foot. As it was, he merely bowed and left the room, amidst general cheering and expressions of good wishes.

When Gerald Hardinge left the tavern, with his brain on fire and his heart aching within him, he felt the necessity for solitude and self-examination; and accordingly skirting the wharves on the edge of the Wexe, and crossing by the lower railway station, made the best of his way to the gardens of North-Hedge. These gardens, given up during the day to nurse-maids and their charges, and to feeble valetudinarians of both sexes, who, screened by large banks of greenery from the cutting winds, sit idly watching the

railway traffic beneath them, are closed at
sundown, and supposed to be deserted during
the night. In the earlier days, however, of
his sojourn at Wexeter, Gerald had often
used them as a short cut from one part of
the town to the other; and recollecting a
gate which could be scaled with tolerable
ease, he proceeded to climb it, and speedily
flung himself down on one of the benches
which nestle under the avenue of broad elms
intersecting the garden. The business carried on at the railway station at Wexeter
has apparently been affected by the general
quietude of the place; there are but two pas-
senger trains during the night, and the goods
traffic is very limited, so that the station
upon which Gerald Hardinge was looking
down lay hushed in repose, and, save by the
sighing of the night winds through the trees,
the silence around him was unbroken.

This was as he wished it. The thoughts
which racked him might be too deep for con-
cealment, and he would have had no human
eye to play the spy upon such consequences

as would result from his contemplated ana-
lysis of his own feelings, and the determination which he would then arrive at. To
stop a ribald laugh, to controvert the effect
of a sneer upon a woman whom he had loved,
he had in the heat of the moment publicly
assumed a position, the retention or resignation of which, fraught with the deepest interest as it would be on his future life, must
be determined upon at once.

A woman whom he had loved ! Was he,
then, to think of as past and bygone that
passion which thrilled his soul and tingled
in his veins, when he held Madge in his arms
but a few short hours previously; as faded
and vanished that love-lit light which had
cast its glamour over the ordinary occurrences of every-day life, and steeped them all
in roseate hues ? Was the temple of his love
so fairy a fabric that at an idle or a lying
word uttered by a gossip it should suddenly
collapse, burying in its ruins the idol which
he had set up therein and worshipped so tenderly ? An idle or lying word ? No, to the

tale told by that wretched old man neither
of these terms could be applied.

Alas! what Gerald did know tallied completely with what Mr. Snick had said. It
was on the night of the thunder-storm that
he had called at Madge Pierrepoint's lodging, and found her absent, attending, as her
sister Rose had told him, to a business engagement. He recollected how he had waited
for her, patiently walking up and down the
street, heedless of the raging elements, and
how he had seen her return at a late hour.
He recollected how he had accused her the
next day of having been to meet some man,
and how, without positively denying it, she
had put aside the question in her soothing
way. And all that time, while he was waiting for her in the storm, not even with a
hope of speaking to her, and going away as
it might be almost contented when he had
seen her safely shut within her own door, she
had been to meet another man, who 'stooped
and put his arms round her and kissed her'!
Gerald remembered the exact words which

Mr. Snick had used, and cursed him aloud for using them.

And yet, in the full knowledge of her treachery and deceit, he had acknowledged her before them as his affianced wife! His affianced wife! That was the position that he had publicly declared her to hold; that was the position that she actually held; for from her manner that evening, her last words, her parting touch, Gerald had but little doubt as to Madge's answer to his appeal. His affianced wife! who went to meet another man in secret, and refused to give him, who would have died for her, any account of her proceedings on that eventful evening.

Now what was he to do? The idea of withdrawing the proposal which he had made, of breaking away from the compact which, as he imagined, was virtually agreed upon between them, never entered into Gerald's mind. What he had said to Madge Pierre-point was, according to his view, quite sufficient in itself to bind him, without taking into consideration the quasi-public announce-

ment which he had made. And this act of
hers—the meeting with this unknown man
—took place before he had actually proposed
to her, and while she was yet a free agent.
What was he to do? He must go through
with it, carrying the burden which he had
laid upon his own shoulders as best he might.
He would see Madge the first thing in the
morning, tell her exactly what had occurred,
repeat the story as it had been told to him,
and ask her what she had to say in her defence. She would be truthful in her reply
—he had an innate conviction of that—and
then he should know what to decide. If she
acknowledged that there was a foundation for
Mr. Snick's story—and it seemed impossible
to think that anything so circumstantial could
be the work of mere invention—where would
be that happiness in the future which he
had so joyfully pictured to himself?

He would keep his word; she should have
nothing to complain of on that score : he
would marry her, and take her away with
him to London; but as to living with her,

that could never be. If she had deceived
him then, with what confidence could he trust
his honour to her keeping when surrounded
by flatterers and tried by temptation! No;
that is the only course open to him, and the
one that he must follow, provided always that
their manner of living can be kept a secret
from the world. If the secret of his betrayed
trust, of his blighted life, were once known,
Gerald felt that the exposure would kill him.
Those were the only terms he would exact
from Madge: that it should be a life-long
secret between them, and so long as she kept
to them, she should share his income, and
be left to do as she pleased. And having
settled this in his own mind, Gerald rose from
his seat, and made the best of his way home.

When he arrived at his lodging, he let
himself in with his key, and was proceeding
straight to bed, when, thinking he saw a light
in the sitting-room occupied conjointly by
himself and Mr. Dunsany, he opened the door,
and discovered that worthy stretched at full
length on the sofa, and snoring in a remark-

ably resonant manner. Gerald was about to
retire quietly, when a snore of extra power
awoke the sleeper, and Mr. Dunsany, rubbing
his eyes, sat upright, apparently considerably
refreshed by his slumber.

'Come in, Gerald,' he cried; 'and don't
be after scuttling off to bed like that, when I
have been sitting up here broad awake, and
denying myself natural sleep, for the chance
of a talk to you. I went straight to your
room directly I got back; and, finding you
were not there, I determined to sit up on the
chance of catching you before you turned in,
as I have something very important to say to
you.'

'Say away, then,' said Gerald, throwing
himself listlessly into a chair, and plunging
his hands into his pockets; 'say away; I'm
listening.'

'Listening!' echoed Mr. Dunsany, who
had gone to a little sideboard, and placed
some bottles and glasses on the table. 'But
I want you to talk as well; and, with a view
to that, hadn't you better put a pipe in your

mouth? I have no hopes of improving your accent, which is essentially English and bad; but tobacco is a great tranquilliser, and brings out the philosophy in a man's nature; and that is a quality of which you have decidedly no superfluity.'

'It is a quality which all of us require more or less,' said Gerald; 'and most of us more.'

'Don't be sneering, and going in for the Diogenes business, my dear Gerald,' said Mr. Dunsany, who, meanwhile, had mixed himself a tumbler of grog, and lighted a large pipe; 'it's not natural to you, I know; but you are upset and worried just now.'

'I am utterly miserable, Dunsany,' said Gerald with a groan.

'Don't say that, my dear lad, for heaven's sake!' cried his friend. 'I've made a good many blunders in my time; but I never made a greater than when I persuaded you to come to that confounded supper to-night, or when I permitted that preposterous old idiot Snick to tell that cock-and-bull story.'

Gerald raised his head, and looked up earnestly.

'You don't believe that story?' he asked.

'Which part of it?' asked Mr. Dunsany.

'Any part,' said Gerald.

'Which part would you wish me to believe?' asked Mr. Dunsany. 'I am open to conviction, my dear lad, and I will oblige you to the best of my ability.'

'Don't be fooling, Dunsany! It is scarcely a subject for jest. Give me a plain answer, if you can.'

'My dear Gerald. the question is rather a complicated and a delicate one, and I wanted to deal with it as delicately as I could. It resolves itself into this: do I believe that a certain lady, a common acquaintance of ours, went on a certain evening, memorable as the occasion of the thunder-storm, up the Dumpington-road, and, in a lane near the turnpike, was met and embraced by a gentleman? Is that the question, or, rather, one of the questions?'

'It is.'

'Well, then, upon my honour, I do believe
it! In the first place, I do not think that old
Snick has the power of inventing anything at
all, much less anything so circumstantial as
that story was in its details of ginger-beer,
turnpike, tollman, and all the rest of it; and,
in the next place, I have noticed, for the last
few days, a certain absence of mind and pre-
occupation of manner in the lady in question.
Now, as to the other part of it: do I believe
that one Gerald Hardinge was the gentleman
who met the lady in the lane near the Dumpington turnpike? Upon my conscience, I do
not. Now, am I right?'

'So far as I am concerned, you are quite
right,' said Gerald, with a heavy sigh.

'Exactly,' cried Mr. Dunsany; 'and it
was a fine manly thing of you to dash in as
you did, my dear lad, and endeavour to save
a lady's character, which was being roughly
handled. Only, like most other spirited and
inexperienced persons, you went too far, and
you proved too much. Why the deuce couldn't
you content yourself with vindicating Miss

Pierrepoint's character, without asserting that she is your affianced wife?'

'I said so because it is the fact,' said Gerald quietly.

'The devil it is!' cried Mr. Dunsany with a long whistle; adding, after a little pause, 'that quite alters the case. You should have told me that before you asked me my opinion.'

'It was scarcely a subject you would have expected me to joke upon,' said Gerald.

'No,' said Dunsany, 'not to joke; but when a point is stretched here it may easily be stretched there. However, it's no use for us to be beating about the bush in this way. You say you are utterly miserable. I have been your chum as yet, and, as a man who is older than you, and has had much more experience of the world, I want to see what can be done to help you.'

'Nothing can be done,' said Gerald moodily; 'nothing.'

'Bah, nothing!' said Mr. Dunsany. 'Now let us see how the land lies. You say you are engaged to Miss Pierrepoint?'

'Well, not exactly engaged. I have asked her to become my wife.'

'And she has not replied?'

'Not exactly.'

'Faith, that's a fine sort of engagement,' said Mr. Dunsany; 'like my countrymen's reciprocity, all on one side.'

'What I mean is, she has not replied in so many words,' said Gerald; 'but there is no doubt of her understanding the offer I made her, and of her accepting it—unfortunately.'

'And why unfortunately?'

'Do you ask me that after having heard Mr. Snick's story?'

'To the devil with Mr. Snick and his story,' said Mr. Dunsany. 'When did you lay your title and lands at Miss Pierrepoint's feet?'

'I asked her to become my wife to-night, not half an hour before I met you.'

'To-night!' echoed Mr. Dunsany. 'And you are grizzling your head off because she chose to meet somebody a few nights ago.'

'But she knew that I was fond of her then,' pleaded Gerald.

'Knew that you were fond of her! A young lady of her beauty and powers of fascination must know that there are hundreds of men who are fond of her, but she cannot be expected to reserve her hand for any one in particular, unless he asks for it.'

'No, certainly, but—'

'But me no buts, as I have no doubt Hayward says in his five-act tragedy, which Miss Pierrepoint would not play. Seriously, Gerald, you are making a donkey of yourself. Instead of being ready to jump out of your skin with delight at the fact of being about to be married to one of the prettiest and cleverest young women possibly to be met with, you are crooning over a cock-and-bull story of her having met some one else some time before you did her the honour to propose to her.'

'There is something in what you say,' said Gerald, brightening a little.

'Something! There is more than you will ever be able to compass, unless your mind expands a great deal, and that's not likely now that you are going away from us, and

you will lose the chance of my tuition. Besides, take my word for it, that meeting was
not exactly as it was represented by that old
Snick, who is a malevolent little wretch, and
would put the worst construction on anything.
Even you must have sense enough to see that
Miss Pierrepoint is not the sort of woman
likely to allow herself to be mixed up in any
compromising affair.'

'I am afraid there is no question about
the meeting,' said Gerald doubtfully.

'No,' said Dunsany; 'but granted that a
meeting took place, the whole force of it, for
good or for evil, depends upon the person
whom she met.'

'It was a man,' said Gerald.

'No doubt,' said Dunsany; 'even Snick is
not idiot enough to make a mistake in that.
But, as I said before, Miss Pierrepoint is not
the sort of person to make promiscuous assig-
nations, and you may take your oath that this
man was her father, her brother, or something
of that kind.'

'She never spoke to me of any of her relations, except the sister who lives with her,' said Gerald.

'The very reason why she would be more likely to meet them in secret,' said Dunsany. 'When you have known a little more of the profession, my dear Gerald, you will find there are numbers of persons in it, especially the female members, who have relations whom they are very shy of noticing in public. Thus, for instance, Miss Montmorency has picked up a bit of education here and there, has a fine figure and a good voice, and is leading lady on the Worcester circuit; while her papa, who is not called Montmorency at all, but Glubb, keeps a small shop or shed in the New Cut. Her line is light comedy, his is onions and coke. Depend upon it, something of that sort is the case in this instance, and you will be very good friends with the old gentleman some day, and let him supply the Wallsends when you settle in town.'

'Snick said it was a tall man,' said Gerald.

'There is no particular reason that I know of why a father should not be tall,' said Dunsany, 'though most of them do run short and broad. However, this might be the brother, the *Wife's Secret* business. You recollect the play? A brother who has come to grief, and is in hiding, and comes to visit his sister secretly, and is suspected by the husband to be her lover. Just our story, by George! Perhaps Miss Pierrepoint's brother has come to grief, frisked the till, or climbed up behind somebody's back on a bill-stamp, or some ingenious little proceeding of that nature, and is keeping out of the way. Depend upon it, it is something of that kind. Now finish your grog, and get off to bed easy in your mind; you are sure to find it all right in the morning.'

'I shall go round and call upon her the first thing,' said Gerald.

'Do,' said Mr. Dunsany. 'So long as you have a good sleep to-night you may do what you please to-morrow. Well,' he muttered to himself, looking after the young man's departing figure, 'I hope I'm right; I do not think the girl is the sort to play double, particularly with such a frank, honest nature as his. But,

even if it comes to the worst, I have postponed
his misery twelve hours, and it was worth
while sitting up a little later and drinking an
extra glass of grog to do that.'

'And what is the matter with my Susan?'
said Mr. Dunsany, coming down to breakfast
the next morning and meeting Miss Cave on
the staircase. 'Has she come to say that
she can conceal her passion for her Mike no
longer? And has she a carriage and four
outside waiting to convey him to the village
church?'

'Get along with you, do, Dunsany,' said
Miss Cave, grinning. 'I was not looking for
you, but for Mr. Hardinge.'

'As I tapped at Mr. Hardinge's door just
now, he roared out that he was in his bath,'
said Dunsany; 'consequently he is not in a
position to meet my Susan's gaze.'

'Well, then, I will give this letter to you
to take to him. It's from Miss Pierrepoint,
and important I am sure, because she begged
me to bring it to him myself.'

'Right you are,' said Dunsany. And he took the letter to Gerald, whom he found in his dressing-gown. Gerald turned very pale when he saw the writing.

'It's from Madge,' he said.

'I know it,' said Dunsany. 'Miss Cave told me; open it now. It's all right, depend upon it.'

Gerald opened the letter and read it through. Then tossing it to his friend, he fell back in his chair, and buried his face in his hands.

'My poor dear fellow, what can be the matter?' said Dunsany. Then casting his eye over the letter, added, 'By George! old Snick was right after all.'

END OF BOOK THE FIRST.

LONDON: ROBSON AND SONS, PRINTERS, PANCRAS ROAD, N.W.